CLUTTER CAN BE DEADLY

SAGE GARDENS COZY MYSTERY

CINDY BELL

CONTENTS

CHAPTER 1

The afternoon air was charged with excitement. At least, the air around Samantha was. Eddy hadn't seen her so excited about anything in quite some time.

"Can you believe it?" Samantha grinned as she wrapped an arm through Eddy's. "Right here in Sage Gardens!"

"I suppose." Eddy met her eyes. "What's the big deal?"

"The big deal?" Samantha grabbed his hand as she spun away from him and laughed. "They're going to film an episode of one of my favorite shows, right here, in our neighborhood, and you're asking me what's the big deal?"

"It's not like we'll be able to be on it, we'll have

to watch it on television, just like everyone else." Eddy shrugged, then shoved his hands into his pockets. "I just don't want you to get yourself all worked up, just to be disappointed."

"I'm not going to be disappointed." Samantha clapped her hands and smiled. "I'm going to be thrilled. That's why I'm inviting everyone over tonight to watch it on my television. Since they are filming live, it will be like we are right there with them the whole time. You'll come, won't you, Eddy?" She met his eyes.

"Of course." He smiled. "I'd never turn down an invitation from you."

"Good, because I need you to bring some chips." Samantha patted his shoulder, then started off down the sidewalk.

"Sam, wait! What about lunch?" Eddy called out to her.

"Sorry, no time today, I have to get to Jo's!" Samantha waved over her shoulder to him, then continued down the sidewalk.

"All right then." Eddy adjusted his fedora, then frowned. Samantha had herself so wound up that he wondered if she would even have enough energy by the time the evening rolled around, to watch the show. Since their lunch date was canceled, he continued down the sidewalk towards Walt's villa. He needed some of his level-headed, logical attitude to wash away the exuberance Samantha bombarded him with.

"Walt? You in there?" Eddy gave his door a light knock.

"Come in, Eddy. I'm in the kitchen." Walt's voice drifted through the window to him.

Eddy pushed the door open and stepped inside. As usual Walt's villa was spotless, and everything was in the correct place. Eddy followed the scent of lemon tea into the kitchen.

"Afternoon Walt." Eddy sighed with contentment as Walt's neat villa was just the calm environment he needed.

"Afternoon Eddy. Would you like some tea?" Walt turned away from the counter with a tea cup in one hand.

"No thanks, I'm fine. Just needed a quiet place for a few moments." Eddy shook his head.

"Uh oh, is Samantha on the warpath about something?" Walt raised an eyebrow, then took a sip of his tea.

"Not exactly. She's just excited. Very excited. Too excited." Eddy settled in one of the kitchen chairs.

"What about?" Walt joined him on the opposite side of the table. He took another big sip of his tea.

"That show, *How Much is it Worth*, is filming an episode in Sage Gardens tonight." Eddy rolled his eyes, then immediately felt a hot spray strike his face.

"*How Much is it Worth* is filming here?" Walt set down the remainder of his tea, then grabbed a napkin from the table. "Oh Eddy, I'm so sorry! Here, you'd better clean that up."

"Walt!" Eddy grabbed the napkin and wiped at his face. "Did you just spit tea all over me?"

"I couldn't help it, I do apologize. I just got so excited, I had no idea this was happening. So sorry, Eddy." Walt frowned and handed him another napkin. "Would you like some hand sanitizer?"

"No! I would like for you not to have spit tea in my face." Eddy grabbed the second napkin and wiped at his neck and chin. "Gross, Walt."

"You're right it is. Do you know how many germs live in human saliva? About a hundred thousand, and that's a low estimate—"

"Walt!" Eddy groaned. "Please, I don't want to know any more about that."

"Oh good, because I want to know everything about the show being filmed. Why are they coming here, to Sage Gardens?" Walt leaned forward eagerly.

"Apparently, one of our neighbors is a collector. They are coming here to film a collection for a live broadcast. Samantha wants us all at her place tonight to watch it together." Eddy crumpled up both napkins and tossed them across the kitchen into the trashcan.

"Brilliant! How exciting!" Walt grinned.

"Not you, too." Eddy groaned and leaned back in his chair. "Walt, don't you see it's just a scheme to get people to watch their show? So what if the collection is worth something, most people aren't going to sell it, and even if they do, they still have to find someone that is willing to buy it."

"Eddy, it's not about the worth, it's about the time and dedication it takes to create such a unique collection of items. It's not as simple as just going to the store and buying something. These items are often a part of our history, they remind us all of a time in our lives that no longer exists. It's rather poetic when you think about it." Walt smiled.

"There's nothing poetic about tea in the face," Eddy grumbled, then stood up. "I suppose then that you will be at Samantha's tonight?"

"Absolutely, what a generous offer. I will be

there." Walt grabbed a spray bottle and some paper towels and began to wipe the tea off the kitchen table. "I promise not to drink anything for the duration of the show."

"Great, then I guess I can leave my rain slicker at home." Eddy chuckled and gave him a quick nod. "I'll see you later tonight."

"Where are you off to?" Walt watched him head for the door.

"Home. I need some quiet time before I have to put up with anyone else's excitement about the show." Eddy sighed as he pushed the door open, then stepped outside. Perhaps it was a bit of an overreaction for him to be so annoyed by the show, but he thought it took advantage of people. They always went for shock value. Sometimes the collector would be so certain that their collection was worth thousands of dollars, only to be told that it was actually worthless. Where was the fun in that?

Still, when the time came around to head for Samantha's, Eddy grabbed a bag of chips, and headed down the sidewalk in the direction of her villa. He could grumble all he wanted, but he would never miss out on time with his friends. He just hoped that the episode would be as exciting as they expected. He guessed it might be, as he'd seen several vans and trucks drive by his villa, with the name of the show printed on their sides. He started to feel just a twinge of excitement as he wondered which neighbor it was that had managed to get on the show. Whoever it was, had kept it a good secret, as the rumor mill in Sage Gardens ran twenty-four hours a day. Curious enough to be interested, he quickened his pace. When he arrived at Samantha's he found that Walt and Jo were already there.

"Hurry, it's going to start soon!" Samantha grabbed the bag of chips from him and disappeared into the kitchen.

"All right, I'm ready." Eddy winked at Jo who smiled back. "Did you get roped into this, too?"

"I might watch the show now and then." Her eyebrows raised. "It might be a guilty pleasure of mine."

"You too?" Eddy groaned as he sat down on the couch. "I'm surrounded by reality television fans!"

"Just go with it, Eddy." Walt grinned at him.

Samantha made it back into the living room with all the snacks, just in time to see the show begin on the screen.

"Oh, here it comes!" She clapped her hands excitedly as she dropped down onto the couch beside Eddy. "I can't wait to see if we're living near a millionaire!"

"Sam, do they ever really have a collection that's worth that much?" Eddy raised an eyebrow.

"Now and then." Samantha smiled. "It's so amazing to see someone's life change right before your eyes. Shh! It's starting."

As the introduction of the show began to play, the four friends were quiet.

"Tonight, we have with us Shayla Thompson." Harold, the presenter of the show, smiled at a woman who appeared to be in her late fifties or early sixties. "Shayla has been collecting all of her life. Isn't that right, Shayla?"

"Yes, that's right." She smiled nervously.

"Do you know her?" Eddy whispered to Samantha.

"No, shh!" She swatted his arm and leaned forward on the couch.

"Could you tell all of us a little bit about the collection we're here to see tonight? Your collection of steel die-cast toy cars?" Harold looked towards the camera with a smile, then turned back to Shayla.

"I bought the first one on the day I found out I was pregnant with my son, Troy." Shayla flashed a smile in the direction of someone off camera. "I thought he would love to play with it. Over time I just kept buying them. The funny thing is, he never wanted a thing to do with them. He was always a finicky child."

Shayla stepped aside to reveal a large collection of toy cars spread out on a table behind her.

"What a sweet way to start a collection." Harold turned to the camera again with an even wider smile. "Are you ready to find out just how much your collection is worth, Shayla?"

"Oh yes." She clutched her hands together. "I couldn't possibly part with it, but I would like to know what it's worth."

"So would we all, and we'll find out, right after this commercial break." He snapped his fingers and pointed at the camera. As the camera panned across the vast amount of items stacked on shelves and piled up against the walls of Shayla's villa, Jo scooted forward on the couch. She narrowed her eyes as she stared at the screen, then shook her head.

"Do you think it's worth something?" Eddy grabbed a cracker from the tray on the coffee table. "A bunch of old toys?"

"Oh yes, definitely." Walt took a deep breath. "It's remarkable, I've never seen that many steel toy cars in one place before." As the television show returned to the screen, and panned over the entire collection of cars, Walt's eyes widened. He leaned forward on the couch. "Thirty-two. Thirty-two under one roof. And not just any roof, but a roof right here in Sage Gardens. How amazing!"

"Walt, is it really that rare?" Jo settled back against the couch and gazed at the screen. "I've seen some precious items throughout the years, and never once have I looked twice at a die-cast toy car."

"Individual cars aren't nearly as valuable, but this collection, and the condition it is in, is what makes it worth quite a bit. I do hope that she has it insured properly." Walt waved his finger at the television. "It needs to be insured and it needs to be kept in a pristine environment. The way she has it right now, it will eventually get damaged."

"I still say it's going to be worthless." Eddy shook his head. "What is the point of collecting them? When is anyone ever going to play with them again?"

"They're not to play with." Walt clucked his tongue. "Certainly not."

"Then what is the point?" Eddy rocked forward in his seat.

"Oh, settle down, Eddy." Samantha placed one

hand on his shoulder as she stepped up behind him. "Different people value things in different ways. Some would say your old recliner is a piece of junk. But to you it's worth something."

"There is not a thing wrong with my chair." He shifted in his seat.

"You two are a perfect pair." Walt grinned. "You're both a little worn out."

"Excuse me, Walt?" Eddy started to stand up.

"Shh!" Walt waved at him. "We're about to find out how much the collection is worth."

"Wonderful." Eddy sat back down.

All four friends watched as the presenter began to speak again.

"Now Shayla, this isn't your only collection, is it?" He held out the microphone to her.

"Oh no, it isn't. I collect just about everything." Shayla shrugged. "Everything has a use, everything has value."

"I see. Your son told me that you have a collection of old condiment packets in the kitchen, is that true?" Harold grinned.

"Well yes, you never know when you might need a spot of something. It's quite a large collection, actually." Shayla glanced over her shoulder, towards a hallway that was piled nearly to the ceiling with

11

old newspapers. "I could spare a few if you need them."

"Oh, no thanks. I have my own condiment supply." Harold smiled, glanced at the camera with a raised eyebrow, then looked back at Shayla. "Now, Shayla, are you ready to find out just how much your collection is worth?"

"Yes." She wrung her hands as she grinned at him.

"What if it's not worth anything at all?" Harold tipped his head from side to side. "Will you be disappointed?"

"Oh, it could never be worth nothing. It's valuable to me, even if other people don't think so. That's what I try to tell my son all the time. But all he can think about is cleaning. I tell him, you'll take my treasures over my cold, dead body." Shayla laughed.

"Ouch, well, I've got some interesting news for you, Shayla. We've gotten the estimate on your collection. Are you ready to hear it?" Harold held up an envelope.

"Yes! Yes, hurry up!" Samantha jumped up from the couch and huffed. "Why don't they just get to it already?"

"Because they want you to hang on their every

word." Eddy rolled his eyes. "It's called manipulative marketing—"

"Enough!" Walt raised both hands in the air. "Quiet! Everyone! He's opening the envelope."

Silence blanketed Samantha's living room as all four friends leaned towards the television.

"Shayla, as it turns out, the collection that you've maintained over all of these years, that you've held so dear, is worth thirty thousand dollars!"

"Thirty thousand?" Shayla squeaked as she spoke. "Are you joking?"

"No, it's worth that much. You have an amazing collection here. Also, I have a buyer who is ready to purchase the entire collection tonight, if you're willing to sell. Will you, Shayla?" The camera panned away from both Shayla and the presenter, then a commercial began to play.

"Thirty thousand!" Walt sat back against the couch and laughed. "I have to say, I thought it would be a little more than that, but that's still a good amount. Just think what a woman like that could do with thirty thousand dollars."

"Quite a bit." Jo nodded slowly as she stared at the screen.

"Maybe she could hire someone to clean up that heap." Eddy narrowed his eyes. "Did you see how much stuff she had in that place? I'm amazed the walls haven't caved in."

"It is pretty crowded in there." Samantha frowned as she picked up her glass of water from the coffee table. "When all of this is over maybe I should offer to help her clean it up a bit."

"I wouldn't do that." Walt shook his head. "She looks like a hoarder to me. I've seen it before. It's not usually easy to get them to part with their things."

"Remember what she said about her son?" Eddy gestured towards the television. "It sounds like the poor sap has been trying to get her to tidy up for a while."

"Do you think she'll sell?" Jo glanced between the three of them. "Is money enough motivation to make her part with her collection?"

"It's hard to say, but I really don't think so." Walt tipped his head towards the screen. "I guess we're about to find out."

CHAPTER 2

*a*s the television show began again, the camera focused in on Shayla's stricken expression.

"No one said I would have to sell it." Her chin trembled.

"No, no Shayla. You don't have to. But there is an offer on the table. If you're willing to sell your collection tonight, you will get thirty thousand dollars. What would you do with that kind of money?" Harold placed a hand on her shoulder.

"No, I don't want it." Shayla winced, then her eyes filled with tears. "I don't want the money. I just want my collection. You're not going to take it are you? Troy!" She looked off camera. "Troy, don't let them take my cars!"

"It's okay, Mom." A young man stepped into view and wrapped an arm around his mother's shoulders. "It's just part of the show. You don't have to sell the cars." He sighed as the camera zoomed in on the two of them. "She doesn't want to sell them, all right?"

"That's just fine, Shayla. I can't blame you for wanting to keep such a stellar collection." Harold stumbled over his words, clearly surprised by her reaction. He turned back to the camera. "All right folks, that's it for now. Join us next week to find out how much it's worth."

"Wow, that was quite a reaction." Samantha frowned as she pressed a hand against her stomach. "Do you think she's okay?"

"It looked like her son was doing a good job of soothing her." Jo pulled out her phone and began to fiddle with it. "Is that show available on the internet?"

"I guess so." Walt shrugged. "Most of them are these days."

"She must be nuts not to sell a bunch of old toys for thirty thousand dollars." Eddy slammed his fist into his palm and grimaced. "What I could do with that kind of money. Wow!"

"She couldn't possibly sell it, Eddy." Walt looked

over at him, his voice stern. "From her reaction I'd say that she's not capable of selling it. Didn't you notice how many things she has in that house? I bet it's even worse in the rooms they didn't show. I've known people like her before. She'll hold on to every item in that house until the day she dies."

"Even the condiments collection?" Samantha scrunched up her nose.

"It may seem strange to all of you, but to her, it would be like giving up one of her own children. Not having her things, would be like asking her not to breathe." Walt pursed his lips. "We all know I have my quirks. No, I'm not debilitated by them, but some people are." He stood up and picked up the empty glasses from the coffee table. "I'll take care of these, Sam."

"Thanks, Walt." Samantha stood up to collect a few of the snacks scattered around the table. "I still think maybe I should go over there, tomorrow. I'd like to bring her a cake or something. Something to cheer her up. No one should be humiliated like that on television."

"You're such a sweetheart." Jo flashed Samantha a smile as she looked up from her phone. "Actually, I'd love to tag along if you'd be up for it."

"Sure, that would be great." Samantha was

surprised Jo wanted to join her, she usually shied away from those types of things. "What about you boys?" Her gaze bounced from Walt to Eddy.

"No way, I'm not going near that place." Eddy grimaced. "Who knows what might come crawling out of there."

"Eddy." Samantha rolled her eyes. "You're really getting cranky in your old age."

"Actually, Eddy is right. I'd love to see that car collection, but it would be a big risk going inside of that house. The amount of germs, mold, and spores that have likely collected in that small space, well it could give you anything from a headache to a toxic infection. I wouldn't recommend going."

"It's not as if we're going to stay for tea." Samantha shook her head as she carried the snacks towards the kitchen. "She's our neighbor, and I just want to make sure that she's okay."

"I think it's a great idea." Jo slipped her phone into her pocket, then followed Samantha into the kitchen. "What time do you want to go over?"

"I'd say about ten. Some people like to sleep in." Samantha set the snacks down on the kitchen counter. "Thanks for going with me, Jo. I have to admit I'm a little nervous about knocking on the door by myself. Who knows how she might react to guests."

"We'll find out tomorrow." Jo gave her a quick hug. "Thanks for this evening, Sam. I'll see you in the morning." As she headed out the back door, Samantha heard some audio playing from Jo's phone, which was still tucked into her pocket.

"How much is it worth?"

Samantha stared after Jo. Did she like the show so much that she decided to replay it? It seemed a little strange to her, but then Jo did have a knack for antiques. She'd spent a good amount of her life stealing valuable items. Now, she was retired, just like the rest of them, but all of the experiences she had in her younger years were still there.

That night as Samantha settled into bed she thought of Shayla. She imagined that she had lived in Sage Gardens for some time to amass so many things in her villa. And yet Samantha had never met her. Samantha was quite well-known in Sage Gardens and attended most social activities. She thought she had met everyone in the retirement community, or at least knew of them. Was it possible that Shayla was a recluse? If Shayla was a recluse, maybe she was very lonely. Maybe Samantha could become her friend, if she was even willing to open the door.

When Samantha woke the next morning, she got started on the cake right away. She was lost in thought as she pulled the cake out of the oven. The delicious aroma of it wafted through the kitchen.

"Perfect." Samantha set the cake down on the counter to cool. Baking hadn't always been a talent of hers. In fact, she'd burned plenty of cakes before she ever created an edible one. But in retirement she'd been able to take a few cooking classes and had mastered a few recipes, including this cake. In her previous career as an investigative journalist she was always on the go. There was always a new story to chase. She didn't spend a lot of time at home, and ate on the road more often than at a table. She attributed the few extra kilos she carried to that life-style. But now that she had plenty of free time on her hands, she liked being able to take her time and do things she never thought she could.

As Samantha cleaned up the mess from making the cake, she thought about Shayla and her tearful reaction the night before. It was clear that the very thought of selling the collection had upset her. She was lucky to have a son at her side that seemed to care about her needs. The further into her senior years she got, the more Samantha realized how easy it was to lose some things to well-intentioned people. It seemed to her, that once she became a senior citizen, the younger generation decided that she needed decisions made for her. Luckily, she didn't have to worry about that too much. But what about someone like Shayla who might not be as strong as Samantha? If it were not for the presence of her son, she might not be allowed to live so independently. She hated to think of Shayla all alone in that packed villa. She decided that no matter what, she would introduce herself to her that morning. It might not lead to instant friendship, but it would at least be a start.

"Morning Sam." Jo sniffed the air as she stepped into the kitchen. "Oh my, it smells amazing in here."

"Thank you." Samantha grinned. "It's going to take me a few minutes to frost it. Do you want some coffee?" She pointed to the coffee pot. "Feel free, I just made it about twenty minutes ago."

"Yes, yes, yes!" Jo lunged towards the pot. "I didn't get much sleep last night." She grabbed a mug from the cabinet above the coffee pot.

"You didn't? Why not?" Samantha smeared vanilla frosting along the top of the cake. She'd heard of people being allergic to chocolate. Vanilla seemed like the safer choice.

"I just had some things on my mind." Jo poured some coffee into the mug, then took a sip of the hot liquid. She didn't always drink it black, but most of the time the bitter taste was enough to get her mind and energy moving.

"I'm sorry to hear that." Samantha added another swath of frosting, then glanced up at her friend. "Anything you want to talk about?" She studied Jo's expression. It had taken a long time for their friendship to bloom, and although now she considered Jo to be one of her closest friends, she knew that when it came to some things Jo remained guarded.

"Nothing worth talking about." Jo shrugged. "Just one of those nights. I'm sure you have them, too."

"Sometimes." Samantha nodded as she recalled the things that would keep her up at night. Most of her investigations had been pretty cut and dry, but some had led her to very messy places. She'd gotten to see some things she wished she hadn't, though she preferred not to dwell on it. "Just about done here. Do you think I should add something else to it? I'm really not great at putting little flowers on or anything like that."

Samantha bit into her bottom lip as she stared at the cake. Did it communicate that she was a friend, and a neighbor, and wanted Shayla to feel welcome? Maybe that was a lot to ask of a simple, yellow cake with vanilla frosting.

"I don't think so. You've done a nice job on it. It looks and smells delicious." Jo looked over the cake. "I think it's perfect."

"Thanks Jo." Samantha smiled at her, then began to rummage around for the lid to her cake container. "I just hope she even likes cake. You know everyone is on a special diet these days. Maybe she's gluten-free, or maybe she's sugar-free, or maybe she just doesn't like sweets. That's something I really can't comprehend." She finally found the lid and straightened up. "How could anyone not like sweets?"

"I certainly enjoy them." Jo swiped her finger towards the frosting on the cake.

"No, you don't!" Samantha gave her hand a firm whack. "If Walt saw that he'd faint!"

"But Walt's not here." Jo grinned.

"Here." Samantha handed Jo the spatula she'd used to spread the frosting. "This will have to do."

"Thanks." Jo dipped the spatula into her coffee and watched the sugary substance melt. "Mm, that's going to be good."

"Creative, I like it." Samantha winked at her, then washed her hands off in the sink. "Do you think she'll even open the door for us? I can't believe we've never met her. I feel like I know every single person that lives in Sage Gardens, at least well enough to wave and say hello."

"I'm not sure. Especially after last night. She might be afraid that we're there to bother her. But once she sees the cake, I bet she'll be happy to see us." Jo finished the last of her coffee and set the mug and spatula in the sink.

"Don't worry about that, I'll get it when we get back. Let's get going before the cake dries out." Samantha started towards the back door.

"Let me get that." Jo pushed it open for her and held it as Samantha walked down two steps onto the path that led out to the sidewalk.

Sage Gardens sprawled out across well-maintained green grass with three, long, winding roads. The grass was intersected by sidewalks that jutted off in all directions. Some led to the lake that all of the villas were centered around, while others led to neighboring villas, and still others led to the community building and office at the front of the development.

"Her villa is in this direction." Samantha started off down a sidewalk that ran by the lake. "She's about halfway along the lake and then up on the second road."

"You did some research." Jo grinned.

"When don't I?" Samantha laughed. "I do just a little bit of overthinking, don't you think?"

"Oh, I don't know. You have a curious mind and a need to get to the bottom of things. There's nothing wrong with that." Jo gave her shoulder a light nudge, and smiled when Samantha looked in her direction. "Natural talent."

"Maybe, but sometimes it gets me into trouble." Samantha grinned. "What a nice morning. I'm sure it will get hot later, but it's nice right now."

"Yes, it is." Jo took a deep breath.

*a*s Samantha and Jo approached Shayla's villa, Samantha tried to ignore a nervous flutter in her stomach. Would she like the cake? Would she even answer the door? Would she be upset by their visit? There were so many possibilities. Although Samantha tried to maintain a positive attitude most of the time, she struggled with self-doubt that sometimes made her a bit nervous about meeting new people.

"Would you mind knocking, Jo?" Samantha shifted the cake container in her hands.

"Sure." Jo stepped up to the door and gave a firm set of knocks. She peered at the window beside the door. "Do you see anyone in there?"

"Nothing yet." Samantha inched a little closer to

the door and turned her head so that she could listen. "It doesn't sound like anyone is moving around in there." She craned her neck to peer past Jo towards the driveway. "No car, maybe she's not home."

"Quite a few people in Sage Gardens don't own a car. Maybe she just doesn't have one." Jo raised her fist into the air. "Should I knock again?"

"Yes, one more time. I'd hate to see this cake go to waste." Samantha frowned.

"Oh, trust me, it won't go to waste." Jo winked at her, then knocked firmly on the door, again.

Seconds slid by as they both stood silently, waiting for any sign of activity inside of the villa.

"I guess she's not home." Samantha sighed. "Or she's just not answering."

"I could take a peek around the back." Jo met Samantha's eyes with a small smile. "It couldn't hurt, could it?"

"Well yes, it might frighten her if she spots you sneaking around the villa." Samantha looked through the window beside the door. Inside she could see piles of boxes and other items, but no sign of a person. Suddenly, a terrible feeling caused her stomach to twist. "Jo, what if she's not okay in there?"

"What do you mean?" Jo looked through the window as well.

"I saw this movie once where a man was a hoarder, and he died, and no one found him for months. He was buried under all of the stuff in his house. Isn't that horrible?" Samantha shuddered at the thought. "What if all of the excitement last night was too much for her?"

"I'd hate to think that. She's probably just not home." Jo frowned and crossed her long, slender arms. "But maybe I should just take a look, to be on the safe side."

"Yes, I think that you should." Samantha glanced towards the road. "I'll keep an eye out."

"Great." Jo nodded, then crept around the side of the house. When she looked back towards the front porch, she saw Samantha still in the same spot, with the cake container in her hands. Her heart skipped a beat. What if someone spotted her and called the police? After spending some years in prison, and having to jump through hoops while on parole, she didn't ever want to end up there again. But a quick look in the window wouldn't hurt anyone, and she had to know if what she saw the night before was real.

The villa was laid out in the same pattern as her

own. Jo peeked through the window that looked into the bedroom. As expected, there were piles of things in that room as well. One pile was so big it almost blocked the window. She spotted a bed, but there were boxes on top of it. She guessed that Shayla did not spend her nights in the bed. She crept farther along the exterior wall and around behind the villa. It had a back step as did all of the villas, and a kitchen window that overlooked the backyard. As she crept up to the window, she hoped that she would find the woman. Samantha had gone to so much trouble to make the cake, and she knew that her friend would be disappointed if she wasn't able to deliver it to Shayla.

Jo stood on her tiptoes as she peered through the window. The clutter in the kitchen made her head spin. If Walt was there beside her, he probably would have fainted. There were dishes piled so high that it was impossible to tell the sink from the stove. The kitchen table however was clean. Two chairs were positioned at it, one on each side of the table. It struck her as a little odd that it appeared to be the only clean place in the house.

Determined to find some sign of the woman, Jo continued around the other side of the house. A large window ran along the side of the living room, and if the curtains weren't drawn completely, she was sure she would be able to get a good look inside. As she approached the window, she was relieved to see no curtains at all. The living room, which was the room where the television show had been filmed, was spotless. The furniture looked new. The carpet had some stains, but it appeared to have been vacuumed. As her gaze swiveled along the furniture, something caught her attention. A pair of shoes, not far from the recliner. They were soft shoes, probably house slippers. Left there by Shayla, she guessed. Perhaps the recliner was where she slept. She also noticed a purse on the table beside the chair. A purse that probably belonged to Shayla. Why would she leave the house without it? Jo's heart began to pound.

When Samantha first expressed concern for the woman's well-being, Jo had instantly thought her friend was being a little paranoid. But now that she saw Shayla's purse, and hadn't seen any sign of her in the villa, she began to wonder as well. If Shayla was there, and not asleep in her bedroom, or the living room, where else could she be? She hadn't been in the kitchen, either. There was only one window Jo hadn't looked through. A small window, too high for her to see into. The bathroom window.

Jo glanced around the backyard for something to give herself a boost. Not far away she found a bucket. After testing the durability of the plastic, she guessed that it would hold her. With her heart still pounding she set the bucket in the grass under the bathroom window. Although she'd spent many years as a thief, she still respected people's privacy. Most of the time if she broke into a home or business it was when no one was there. On occasion she had thought no one had been inside the premises, but she was wrong. She braced herself for what she might see when she looked through the window, and the possibility that she might get caught. Of all the things she imagined she might see when she peered through the open window, the one thing she didn't expect was a clean and empty bathroom. Everything appeared tidy, and there was no sign that anyone had used it recently.

"Another empty room," Jo muttered to herself and narrowed her eyes. "Where are you, Shayla?" She walked back around to the front of the villa and found Samantha still in the same spot that she'd left her. "I'm sorry, I didn't see anyone inside." She rubbed the back of her neck beneath her long, black ponytail. "Her purse was there, though."

"Maybe she went out for a walk?" Samantha scanned the sidewalks that led away from the villa.

"Maybe." Jo wrapped her arms around herself, and shivered. "Something just doesn't feel right."

"That's what I thought earlier." Samantha frowned. "Maybe I should try the door? Just to see if it's unlocked?"

"It couldn't hurt." Jo nodded, then watched as Samantha reached for the doorknob. When she turned it, the knob twisted, but the door didn't swing open.

"It's unlocked, but—" Samantha gave the door a firm push, then she looked down at the corner of it. "Oh, there's something wedged in it." She gave it another hard shove with her shoulder, and the door became dislodged.

"She must be inside." Jo caught Samantha's arm before she could step through the door. "If the door was stuck, then she didn't just open it to go for a walk."

"She could have used the back door." Samantha's voice wavered.

"She could have." Jo nodded. "Why don't you let me go in first?"

"Should we even go in?" Samantha hesitated as

she stepped away from the door. "Maybe we should just call the police."

"What if it's nothing?" Jo shook her head. "We have no idea if there's actually an emergency. Just let me take a quick look around, and if she's there then I'll make sure she's okay."

"All right, but I'm coming with you." Samantha stepped in behind her.

"Shayla?" Jo called out as she picked her way through the packed hallway. "Shayla, are you home?"

"How is it going to look that we have never met this woman. but now we're in her house?" Samantha sighed.

"Be careful, Sam. Some of these piles don't look very stable." Jo edged her way around a stack of books and magazines. "Shayla? Are you here? We're here to help! Call out if you're here!"

As Jo passed one particular spot, she stopped and looked through all of the items piled up on a shelf. The item she expected to see, wasn't there. She narrowed her eyes, looked for a moment longer, then continued down the hallway. The farther down the hallway she went, the less cluttered it became. She noticed that everything had been cleared away in

CINDY BELL

front of one door. She knew what door it was, she had the same door in her villa. It was a storage closet. Could Shayla be hiding inside? She reached for the knob in the same moment that she took a deep breath. As the door started to open, she found it to be heavier than expected. A second later she realized why. Something had been leaning against it. She gulped as she gazed down at Shayla. She'd been wedged inside the closet, and though there were no outward signs of injury, it was clear that she had passed away.

CHAPTER 4

Samantha gazed at the piles upon piles of items that sprawled down half of the hall-way. Dazed by the sight of it, she couldn't look past it.

"Samantha!" Jo gasped as she stumbled a few steps back in the hallway.

"Jo, shh, don't shout." Samantha hissed as she turned in her friend's direction. "Someone will catch us in here."

"Sam, we're way past that." Jo fumbled in her pocket for her cell phone.

"What is it?" Samantha, startled by the panic she heard in Jo's voice, edged closer to her. As she peered around Jo's arm, she caught sight of the bare feet that stuck out of the bottom of the closet. "Oh no! Oh no!" She started to push past Jo to check on the woman's well-being, but Jo caught her around the waist before she could.

"Don't, she's long gone, Sam. There's nothing we can do for her." Jo took a breath. "We should call the police."

"Yes. I'll call. I'll do it." Samantha pulled her cell phone from her pocket and turned back towards the front door. She pushed open the door with her phone pressed against her ear and walked right into someone who stood outside. "Oh! Excuse me!" Samantha's heart lurched with fear as she gazed into the eyes of a strange man, who glared straight back at her.

"What are you doing in there?" His scowl darkened even further when he heard Jo call out from inside.

"Samantha! Did you get through, yet?"

"We need help out here in Sage Gardens!" Samantha rattled off the address of the villa as she slipped between the door and the man who hadn't budged an inch.

"What's going on here?" The man shoved past Samantha and pulled the door open far enough for him to step inside. "You get away from there! You have no business in my wife's things!"

"Sir, wait!" Samantha followed him through the door, as Jo spun on her heel to face him. "I'm sorry, but something terrible has happened." Samantha caught him by the shoulder before he could lunge at Jo. "Please, come back outside."

"Something terrible?" He looked between the two of them.

Jo stood in front of the closet, but her slender frame didn't do much to hide Shayla's body.

"Shayla's your wife?" Samantha did her best to guide him back towards the door, however he pulled against her hand and craned his neck to see past Jo.

"Yes, she is. Well, we're not together anymore, but legally we're still married." He frowned. "I have more right to be here than you do. Now, let me past!"

Sirens began to ring out not far from the villa.

Samantha noticed increased tension in the man's shoulder as she grasped it.

"What's happened?" He shoved her hand away and pushed past her into the hallway.

"I'm afraid she's gone." Jo spread her shoulders wider as he approached her. "We've just found her, and she's passed away."

"What?" His knees buckled, and he leaned one

hand against the wall beside him. "Is this some kind of joke?"

"No, it isn't." Samantha walked up behind him. "I'm sorry for your loss, sir."

"Jacob." He cleared his throat. "My name is Jacob."

"I'm sorry for your loss, Jacob," Samantha said gently. "Come outside, let the police sort all of this out. You don't want to see her like this."

"Yes, you're right, I don't." He allowed Samantha to guide him back towards the door, though his body trembled as she did. When they reached the door, two police officers greeted them.

"We got a call to this address?" The taller of the two looked into Samantha's eyes.

"Inside. There's been a death." Samantha clenched her teeth to hold back her reaction to speaking those words.

"How could this happen?" Jacob sank down onto the top step of the porch and hung his head. "She was healthy, I know she was."

Samantha bit into her bottom lip. She wasn't sure how much to say. Did she want to point out to him that it was very unlikely that Shayla had tucked herself into a closet to die? She guessed that this death hadn't been natural causes. She believed it was a murder.

"I'm sure the police will figure out what happened." Samantha brushed her hair back from her eyes as a terrible feeling crept over her. She and Jo had discovered the body. They hadn't just discovered it, they had broken into the house and found it. What explanation would she give to the police?

"What's that?" Jacob tilted his head towards the container that she'd left on the porch.

"A cake. I made Shayla a cake." Samantha's voice shook. The morning had started off with such good intentions, and now the cake was just a reminder that Shayla was gone.

"Shayla never mentioned any friends in the area. She was a recluse." Jacob stared at her. "Why did you make her a cake?"

"I didn't know her." Samantha cleared her throat. "But I saw her on television last night. I just thought she might need some cheering up."

"Or you thought you could take advantage of her?" Jacob narrowed his eyes. "Maybe you planned to give her the cake and see what you could steal? Or take pictures of the way she lived?"

"I would never do either of those things."

Samantha glared back at him, then reminded herself that he had just lost someone he cared about. "I should speak with the police."

Samantha stepped forward just as Jo was escorted out the door by the shorter of the two officers.

"Sam, this is Officer Dupree, he wants to talk to you about everything that happened this morning." Jo's normally confident expression had been replaced by one of thinly veiled horror. Samantha knew it wasn't about Shayla's death. It was about being questioned by the police.

"Sure, yes, I'll speak to him. Jo, maybe you should head home, let Eddy and Walt know what happened." Samantha took her hand and looked into her eyes. "I'll be fine."

"Can I?" Jo shot a fearful look in the direction of the officer.

"Yes, in a few minutes. Let me just question Samantha and make sure nothing else needs to be covered. It won't take long. After that, if there's nothing else we have your contact information, the detective on the case will be in touch." The officer nodded.

Jacob stood up.

"Detective? Why is there going to be a detective

involved in all of this?" He pushed past Samantha to get to the officer. "What's happened to my wife?"

"Sir, it appears that there has been a homicide." The officer met his eyes. "I'm very sorry for your loss. An investigation will be opened, as of now this villa is a crime scene. I will have to ask all three of you to please step off the porch and out to the perimeter of the property so that we can begin to collect evidence."

"A homicide?" Jacob stumbled back a few steps. "You're saying that someone killed Shayla?"

"I'm afraid so." He pulled a notebook from his pocket. "Why don't you and I talk about a few things." He led Jacob down off the porch and onto the front lawn. The officer spoke into his radio then turned to Samantha. "My partner will be out in a minute to interview you."

"This is terrible." Jo picked up the cake container, then she and Samantha descended the steps. They waited on the grass for Samantha to be interviewed.

A few minutes later the taller of the officers exited the villa and introduced himself to Samantha. She gave her details and a description of what had happened. Then she and Jo were told they could leave. They walked towards the street.

"Who could have done this to her?" Samantha looked back over her shoulder at the officer whose attention was still focused on Jacob.

"Samantha!" Eddy called down the street.

Doors began to swing open on the villas up and down the street. The flashing police lights, and the commotion on the front lawn had drawn the attention of curious Sage Gardens' residents. It wouldn't be long before the entire community found out what happened. Samantha headed towards Eddy as he approached her.

"Oh Eddy!"

"What's happened?" He looked between her and Jo, then settled his gaze on the police officers.

"I just came over to give her a cake." Samantha pointed at the cake container.

"Shayla's been murdered." Jo clutched the cake container in her hands as she stared at Eddy. "We found her."

"Seriously? Murder?" Eddy stared into Jo's eyes for a moment.

"Yes." Jo lowered her eyes. "There's no question about it."

"Sam, are you okay?" Eddy turned his attention back to her, and looked into her eyes.

"I'll be fine." She nodded. "I'm just glad we

found her. What if we hadn't gone inside, Eddy? What if no one had? What if she wasn't found for weeks?"

"We did." Jo took a deep breath. "That's all that matters. I'm going to go tell Walt what happened, before he hears it from someone else. He knew I was going with you to deliver the cake, he'll be worried."

"Okay." Samantha nodded. "I guess I should throw that out." She stared at the cake container.

"I'll take it home. You can decide later what you want to do with it." Jo managed a small smile.

"Thanks Jo." Samantha leaned towards Eddy again, relieved to be surrounded by people who cared about her. "Eddy, what if we had gotten there sooner. Maybe we could have saved her."

"Don't think about that now," Eddy said softly. "The important thing is that you found her, and now we're going to be able to figure out what happened to her."

"Are we?" Samantha asked. "Eddy, that poor woman. To think she was just on television last night, and this morning she's dead." She shivered. "Who would do such a thing?"

"Yes, she was on live television last night." Eddy frowned as he tilted his head in the direction of the villa. "It seems to be a little too coincidental to me that she would be on the show last night, and dead this morning. I bet it had something to do with her being on the show."

"Maybe. But why would anyone want to kill her over some antiques?" Samantha pressed her hand against her chest. "Maybe the murderer stole her car collection?"

"Maybe." Eddy narrowed his eyes. "It could have been the motive, and perhaps Shayla surprised the thief. Who is that?" Eddy looked towards the man and the officer on the front lawn.

"Jacob. He said he is Shayla's husband. They were separated, apparently. He showed up right after we found Shayla's body." Samantha straightened her shoulders, determined to remain strong.

"Showed up?" Eddy watched the man. "Out of the blue?"

"It seemed that way." Samantha followed his gaze.

"Or maybe he was already there, but didn't want you and Jo to know that?" Eddy rubbed his hand along his chin as his eyes followed the interaction of the officer and Jacob. "It seems too coincidental to me." With a gentle grasp on her shoulders he started to steer her away from the villa. "Let's get you home so you can rest a bit. This is a lot to handle."

"Maybe we should stay." Samantha craned her neck in order to look back in the direction of the villa. "There might be some evidence we can find. Something that could give us an idea of what happened to Shayla."

"Now isn't the time." Eddy gave her shoulder a subtle squeeze. "The police are going to want to conduct a thorough search, and hanging around here is only going to interfere with their investigation."

"But Eddy, someone did this, someone went into her villa and killed her. Who knows how long ago it happened. That killer could still be roaming loose in Sage Gardens." Samantha pulled away from him and started back towards the villa.

"Not now." Eddy caught her hand with his. "Stop, please." He tipped his head in the direction of a car that pulled up into Shayla's driveway.

Samantha watched as Shayla's son, Troy, stepped out of the car.

"Dad?" He started up the driveway. "What's going on here? Why are you here? Why are the police here?"

"Oh Troy." Jacob shook his head slowly as he

stared at his son. "I have some difficult news for you."

"Difficult news? You don't even have the right to be here. What kind of lies are you telling these officers? Did Mom call the police? Were you harassing her?" Troy pushed back his father's attempt at restraining him from the porch. "Mom?" He called towards the villa. "Mom? Are you okay?"

Samantha shivered as she thought of the horrible news that Troy was about to be given. It was clear that there was some animosity between him and his father. Would he have anyone to comfort him and help him through the loss of his mother? In that instant Samantha decided that the best thing to do to help him was to help find out who did this to his mother.

"Come with me, son." Jacob's grave expression hinted that perhaps he understood just how dire the moment would be for his son. "We need to talk."

"I don't want anything to do with you!" Troy marched straight towards the police officers. "Someone needs to tell me what is going on here."

"We should go, Sam." Eddy steered her away from the driveway, and this time she didn't resist. The moment was a personal one. Not one to be watched by a couple of strangers.

"I'm going to find out everything I can about what happened. I know you want to solve this. I know that you're going to have a lot of questions, Sam, and we will find some answers."

"Thank you, Eddy." She smiled slightly.

"We'll figure this out in no time." He winked at her, then gestured towards the villa ahead of him. "Stay with Walt and Jo. I'll bring back any information I can get."

"All right." Samantha took a deep breath, then looked into his eyes. "Thanks for caring, Eddy."

"Aw, stop, you're going to ruin my reputation." Eddy flashed her a grin.

Samantha rolled her eyes, then headed for Walt's villa. As she walked, she could feel Eddy's eyes on her. She knew that he wouldn't look away until she'd reached the safety of Walt's villa. Eddy could joke about how tough he was, how detached from the rest of the world he was. But she knew from the way he lingered to make sure that she was safe, that he cared far more than he'd ever admit.

CHAPTER 5

*E*ddy decided that the best place to start was by talking to Owen, the nurse at Sage Gardens. He quickly walked the short distance along the lake towards Owen's office with a heavy heart, and his thoughts on the woman he'd seen on television the night before. He knocked on Owen's door. A few seconds later it swung open to reveal a woman who looked to be in her fifties with short, brown hair. She smiled slightly.

"Can I help you?" She stared at Eddy inquisitively.

"I'm looking for Owen," Eddy explained.

"He has a few days off. What do you need?" Her expression didn't change. "Are you sick?"

"No." Eddy shook his head. He thought about

asking the woman about Shayla, but decided against it. He had never seen her before so he doubted she even knew her, or that she would reveal information about her if she did. "I just needed to speak to Owen."

"Okay." She shrugged and closed the door.

Eddy turned on his heel. He knew the detective on the case could be the best place to find information and wanted to speak to him as soon as possible. It would take time for the detective to review the crime scene, but Eddy hoped he might already have some information to share.

As Eddy walked back down the street towards Shayla's villa, he stopped to chat to a couple of the residents milling about in the street discussing what had happened. He wanted to see if they knew anything about the murder.

Not only did they not know anything more than what Eddy knew about that morning's events, neither had met Shayla. They only knew of her from the show the night before. He wondered if anyone in Sage Gardens had even met Shayla.

Shayla's villa was surrounded by police cars when he arrived.

Eddy looked at the few officers who were outside and smiled when he recognized one of the officers. Then he remembered that this officer played strictly by the book and would not give Eddy any information about the case.

"Johnny." Eddy held out his hand as he walked over to him.

"Eddy." The officer smiled and took his hand.

"I was wondering if I could please speak to the detective on the case."

"You could, but you just missed him," Johnny explained.

"Oh?" Eddy frowned.

"Yes, Detective Cooper had to go back to the station, but he won't be long." Johnny smiled. "Can I help you with anything?"

"Can you give me any information about what happened here?" Eddy knew he had pretty much no chance of getting any information from him, but it was worth a shot.

"Eddy, you know I can't." He shook his head.

"Okay." Eddy nodded to him and turned away. He would try and speak to the detective at the station. He would probably have more chance of getting some time alone with him there.

Eddy walked back to his car and headed straight to the police station. One of his friends at the police department, Detective Brunner was on vacation and

Detective Cooper had only recently transferred in. Eddy wasn't sure that the detective would be very responsive to his questions about the crime. He hoped he might pay him the professional courtesy of revealing what the investigation had turned up so far, but he couldn't be certain that he would.

As Eddy stepped into the police station, he noticed that it was fairly crowded. With a local festival in full swing he guessed that there were a few issues the police were dealing with. A visit from a retired cop, might not be received well. The officer at the front desk waved to him as he approached.

"Hey Eddy, what can I help you with?"

"Things are hopping around here, huh?" Eddy swept his gaze over the crowded lobby, then looked back to Michael, an officer he knew fairly well.

"Nothing too serious, just a lot of nuisance issues. And of course, what happened out in Sage Gardens." He arched an eyebrow as he stared at Eddy. "I guess that's what you're here for?"

"Yes. I thought maybe I could speak with the new detective. Cooper, isn't it?" Eddy glanced past the front desk, towards the tangle of desks and cubicles beyond it. "Do you think that he'd be willing to see me?"

"He might." Michael lifted one shoulder in a

mild shrug. "He's not a bad guy, but this is a big case for him to handle after only being here for a short time. Let me check." He punched a button on the phone beside him, then picked up the handset. As he spoke into the phone, Eddy watched the desks beyond him in an attempt to guess which one belonged to Cooper. "All right." He nodded as he hung up the phone. "Detective Cooper will see you, but he's with someone in interrogation room one right now, so you're going to have to wait." He gestured to the crowded lobby. "Ah, you know what? Just go on back. There's a bench in the hall-way, you can wait there for him."

"Great, thanks Michael." Eddy headed past the large desk and down the first hallway. Although the doors were unmarked, he knew they each led to an interrogation room. He had to wonder if Detective Cooper already had a suspect. If so, at least he could give Samantha some good news. After a few minutes, a door farther down the hallway swung open, and a man who looked to be in his thirties, followed by another man who looked to be in his sixties, stepped out.

"I appreciate your time." The younger man gave the older man's hand a firm shake. "I know it was an inconvenience for you, but your insight has been invaluable."

"Anything I can do to help." The older man nodded. His dark eyebrows knitted together over sharp, green eyes. "Shayla certainly didn't deserve this."

"No, she didn't." The younger man shook his head. When he caught sight of Eddy on the bench, his eyes narrowed briefly, then he directed the older man towards the exit of the building. "I'll be in touch if I have any more questions."

"Anytime." The older man nodded to Eddy as he walked past him.

Eddy nodded back, then stood up and turned towards the younger man.

"Detective Cooper?"

"That would be me." He slid his hands into the pockets of his suit pants. "You must be Eddy?"

"I am." He braced himself for a quick dismissal.

"I've heard about you. John Eddy Edwards." He smiled some. "You have quite the reputation around here."

"A good one I hope." Eddy attempted a weak smile.

"Quite the reputation." The detective cleared his

throat. "Do you want to come in?" He pushed the door to the interrogation room open.

"In there?" Eddy hesitated.

"I assumed that you would want to speak in private."

"Sure, private would be good." Eddy nodded, then stepped through the door into the interrogation room. When he heard the door click closed behind him, he spun on his heel and found Detective Cooper just inside the door.

"Have a seat." Detective Cooper gestured to one of the two chairs at the table.

"Don't you want to know why I'm here?" Eddy walked around the side of the table, but didn't sit. It seemed to him that the detective was up to something.

"I know why you're here." Detective Cooper grabbed the other chair and spun it around. As he straddled it, he looked straight at Eddy. "You live in Sage Gardens, there was a murder in Sage Gardens this morning. You're here to stick your nose into things."

"No offense intended." Eddy held up his hands. "I don't want to overstep. I just thought I might be of some help to you. I know you're new to the area, and I've been in Sage Gardens for some time. I thought maybe I could give some advice or direction on different questions you might have."

"Do you know who the killer is?" The detective's lips twitched upward in a slight smile. "That would be very helpful."

"Sorry, no. But it seems like you're on the right track." Eddy tipped his head towards the door. "You already brought in a suspect?"

"A suspect, not exactly." Detective Cooper rested his arms on the top of the chair. "Shayla had a rather interesting life."

"Did she?" Eddy leaned forward some. "I never had the chance to know her."

"Yes, she's been questioned by the police before." He tapped his fingers along the top of the chair. "Eddy, I'm not opposed to sharing some information with you. However, I expect information to be shared in return. Deal?" He locked his eyes to Eddy's.

"Yes, whatever information I can give to help you, I'd be happy to." Eddy studied the man across from him.

"Shayla was arrested once before. About fifteen years ago. She was a suspect in a crime, a murder. She was a suspected accomplice." He shrugged.

"The charges were later dropped, because the person she was meant to have helped was cleared."

"Oh well, that settles that then." Eddy frowned.

"It seemed to. Anyway, when I found this in her file, I called in the man who was arrested alongside her at the time. He was arrested for the murder, but the charges were dropped as he had a solid alibi. I was just curious about whether he might still have been in contact with her and if there's any information he could tell me. It's not exactly common to be involved in a murder investigation so I thought I should look into it." He squinted at Eddy. "What do you think?"

"Well, when you get to be my age, you realize that unusual things do happen. The older a person gets, the more experiences they have, and it sounds like Shayla had plenty." Eddy clenched his jaw as he considered the possibilities. "Had they still been in touch?"

"No, not at all." Detective Cooper sighed as his shoulders drooped. "I had hoped it was going to be a good lead, and all of this could be settled soon."

"That would be for the best." Eddy finally eased down into a chair. "But those first few hours are crucial, you can't get too distracted."

"My thoughts exactly. While I waited for Brad

to come in, I used the time to look over the files of all the residents at Sage Gardens. Well actually, just the ones that have a criminal history." The detective smiled. "Not too many of those, luckily."

"Quite." Eddy's chest tightened.

"As I understand it, you may know one of those residents well." Detective Cooper straightened up in his chair. "Joanne Baylor. You probably know her as Jo?"

"Yes, I know Jo." Eddy's mind spun. Was their entire meeting a plot to get information out of him about Jo?

"She has an interesting history. Some prison time." He tipped his head back. "Is she the violent sort?"

"No, of course not. She had nothing to do with this." Eddy shook his head. "You're wasting your time looking into her."

"It's easy to believe that people change. But in my experience that's not usually the case." The detective stood up from his chair and walked around the side of the table. "I plan to speak to her about her whereabouts last night."

"It's really not necessary. Jo would never do anything to hurt anyone." Eddy looked up at the detective. "You can trust me on that."

"I wish I could, but I barely know you, Eddy. You did agree to give me information, remember? I was thinking, perhaps you could speak to her for me. My guess is being hauled into a police station wouldn't be a good experience for her and she might clam up. I would also guess that she probably wouldn't want to speak to me about anything. So, what do you say? Can you find out the information I need from her?" Detective Cooper flashed Eddy a grin. "It would be so helpful."

"Uh sure, I can talk to her. I'm sure there won't be anything to tell you, though." Eddy stood up from his chair as well. "Have you thought about what the motive might have been? Why someone would want to do this to Shayla? You are aware that she was on a live television show last night?"

"Yes, I'm aware. I'm not sure that the two incidents are related, however. The show didn't reveal her address. But I suppose those of you that live in Sage Gardens would be able to figure that out. Did Jo watch the show last night?" The detective crossed his arms as he looked at Eddy.

"Yes, she did." Eddy swallowed hard. "We all did, my friends and I."

"I see. I'm sure everyone in Sage Gardens did. But it was your friend, Jo, and uh, Samantha, was it, who went to the villa this morning." Detective Cooper began to pace slowly back and forth across the room.

"Yes, it was. Samantha thought Shayla could use some cheering up, as the show ended so awkwardly." Eddy slipped his hands into his pockets. "She baked her a cake, and Jo went with her."

"Interesting. You can see how odd it is to me that one of the few criminals who live in Sage Gardens happened to be at the villa on the morning that Shayla died, can't you? A criminal that used to steal valuable items in a villa possibly packed with some valuable items?" He reached for the door. "Get me Jo's whereabouts after she left Samantha's villa to when she found the body. I'd hate to have to force her to come in here for questioning."

"I will." Eddy stared hard at him. "Leave it to me."

"Okay." Detective Cooper nodded. "I better get back to the crime scene. The evidence is going to take an army to go through."

"More tea, ladies?" Walt stood up from the table and headed in the direction of the kettle.

"One cup is enough, thank you." Samantha pushed away her tea cup.

"I'll take another if you don't mind, Walt." Jo stared down into the remains of her tea.

"What a tough morning." Samantha sighed as she sat back in her chair.

"Do you think Eddy found anything out?" Jo looked over at Samantha.

"I hope so. But it's hard to predict whether the detective will be willing to talk to him." Samantha pursed her lips as she checked her phone. "Still nothing."

"I'm sure that he will call soon." Walt returned with a fresh cup of tea for Jo. He sat down across from the two women and stared down at his hands. "I keep thinking about the show last night, and her beautiful car collection. I wonder. Did someone kill her for the collection? Or for something else that was valuable?"

"I don't know." Samantha sighed. "There were no signs that it was a robbery."

"Actually." Jo cleared her throat. "I wouldn't say that."

"What do you mean?" Walt looked up at her.

"I mean, it would be pretty hard to tell if anything was missing, based on how many things were in that villa. It's not as if the robber would leave much of a mess behind, when the villa is already overrun with piles of junk." Jo took a breath, then looked down at her tea. "I just don't think that robbery should be ruled out."

"It seems like the most reasonable motive, after her collection was featured on television last night. Perhaps the person that made the offer to buy the car collection was frustrated when she rejected it." Walt raised an eyebrow. "I wonder if there is a way for us to find out who that was."

"That's a good question." Samantha picked up her phone. "I'll make some calls and see what I can find out. I still have a few contacts in the entertainment industry." As she walked into the next room, Walt shifted his gaze back to Jo.

"What else did you notice in the villa, Jo?" Walt tapped the side of his own tea cup in a steady rhythm that soothed him as he counted each tap.

"Just a mess, like I said." Jo swirled the tea in her cup.

"Jo." Walt watched the tea near the rim of the cup. "What's going on? You're hiding something from me."

"I'm not." She looked up at him with a sharp gaze. "Why would you say that?"

"I can tell." Walt sat back in his chair, and noticed the way her eyebrows furrowed. It made her eyes just a little darker.

"You're not as observant as you think." Jo waved a hand dismissively. "The place was a wreck."

"What about the car collection? Did you see it?" Walt noticed the nervous tremble in her hand, and the way she tucked it into her lap, as if he might not notice.

"I didn't see it, but I wasn't looking for it." Jo sighed as she looked up at him. "It was a rough morning, Walt, please don't pick me apart."

"Of course." He nodded and offered her a mild smile. "You need time to recover."

Samantha stepped back into the kitchen with her phone in her hand.

"I spoke to the producer of the show, and it turns out the offer to buy the collection actually came from her son, Troy. It was apparently the only way he agreed to be mentioned on the show. He wanted to see if his mother would be willing to sell the collection. He wanted it and hoped it would be a way to get her to start getting rid of some things from the villa." Samantha shook her head as she sat down in an empty chair. "I can't imagine being so manipulative with my own mother."

"But your mother also didn't put her health and the health of others at risk, I'm sure." Walt sighed. "Though it does seem to be extreme that he would do that."

"Hey everyone." Eddy knocked lightly on the screen door as he pulled it open.

"Eddy!" Walt stood up to welcome him inside. "Would you like some tea?"

"Sure Walt, thanks." Eddy headed for the kitchen table.

"Did you find anything out?" Samantha looked up at him.

"A few things, yes." As Eddy filled them in on the information about Shayla's past, his gaze wandered repeatedly to Jo. "And Detective Cooper mentioned that it's going to take an army to go through all of the evidence. Thinking about it on my way here, I decided to text him and suggest that Walt might be able to help, as he's so good with numbers and is able to memorize things." He glanced over at Walt as he handed him a cup of tea. "I hope you don't mind that I volunteered your help."

"I don't mind." Walt smiled. "Did he accept?"

"Yes, I told him you would meet him at Shayla's villa. Of course, you'll have to follow whatever directions the crime scene team give you." Eddy paused. "I could come with you if you'd like."

"No, that's okay. I'll be fine." Walt nodded to Eddy. "I really want to check and see if the car collection is still there and if anything is missing from it."

CHAPTER 6

*A*s Walt left his villa, he felt his heartbeat quicken. It did every time he left his sanctuary. In his villa, everything was exactly as he wanted it. He felt sympathy for Shayla, as although he could never survive in the clutter and mess she lived in, he understood the compulsion to keep things exactly as she needed them to be. Maybe her son had confronted her about the car collection. Maybe things had gotten ugly. He cringed at the thought. When he arrived at Shayla's villa he was escorted inside.

"Walt?" A young man offered his hand. "I'm Detective Cooper."

"Pleasure to meet you, Detective Cooper." Walt

kept his hands clenched together. He tried not to breathe too deeply in the dusty, cramped villa.

"Eddy said you could help me out with this madness." He gestured to the mess around them. "Do you think you can?"

"Yes, but first, I need to see the collection. The car collection." Walt swept his gaze over the collection of items and memorized and cataloged each item in his mind.

"Over here." A young woman with a CSI jacket on gestured to a space between two crowded hallways.

"Thanks."

Walt stared at the collection of steel cars. He counted each one, over, and over again. As he began to pace the length of the room, Detective Cooper watched him.

"Well? What is it? Eddy said you were a genius, but you've been staring at this collection for thirty minutes. Are you going to tell me why?" His bushy eyebrows knitted together over his dark eyes.

"There is a car missing. There were thirty-two cars. Thirty-two in her collection." Walt rubbed his hand along his chin. "Someone must have taken it."

"Why would anyone ever just take one car?"

The detective walked closer to him. "Was there something special about it?"

"No. It is the first car that Shayla bought, but the cars are practically worthless if they're not part of a collection. I have no idea why they would take just one car." Walt began to pace again. "There must have been a reason."

"We don't think this was a robbery. We think there was another motive for this murder. What that motive was, we don't know yet, but we're getting closer." Detective Cooper nodded. "One missing car doesn't mean much. She might have moved it, hidden it away somewhere. It's going to take us weeks to sort through all of the contents of her house, and right now we're in a bit of a battle with her son to stop him from emptying it out."

"He's trying to stop you from collecting evidence?" Walt turned to face the detective with wide eyes. "Why would he do that?"

"I'm not sure. But he keeps insisting that he wants it all cleared out as quickly as possible. I'm assuming it's for the sake of selling the villa. However, unless we are able to take a suspect into custody, we're not going to be able to let him do that." The detective stared at the open file in his hands. "I honestly don't even know where to begin with the evidence."

"Don't worry, I'm here to help." Walt flashed him a smile, then he pulled on a face mask. "We'll have this counted up in no time."

The tension in Walt's villa was thick, and Samantha wasn't exactly sure why. She frowned as she glanced between Eddy and Jo.

"I think it's interesting that Troy was behind the offer to buy the collection." Eddy squinted across the table at Jo as she continued to stare at her phone.

"I think so, too." Samantha nodded slowly. "I also think it's interesting that Shayla was involved in a murder previously."

"Me too." Eddy held up one finger. "She was considered an accomplice at first. I honestly don't know anything about the murder, but I have a few calls out to see if I can get more information about it. This friend of hers, Brad, I'm trying to find out a bit more about him. But Detective Cooper didn't seem to consider him to be of interest." He shrugged. "I do feel a little better that he's taking this seriously, and that he was willing to accept Walt's help. That's a sign of a decent man, if he's willing to accept help."

"I can agree with that." Samantha nodded. She picked up her phone as it began to ring. "Hi Bunny." She sighed as the woman's high-pitched voice began to shriek in her ear. She was wound up about Shayla's death and wanted to know every detail. "I honestly don't have much to tell you, Bunny, I'm sorry." She stood up from the table. "Excuse me, Jo, Eddy." She stepped out of the kitchen into the living room as Bunny went on to describe her plans for a memorial. "Why yes, I do think that's a good idea. I know most if not all of us didn't know her, but I still think it would be good to honor her." She began to make a list on a notepad that Walt had carefully positioned on the table beside the couch. "Sure, I can pick those things up. I honestly have no idea if her son will be there. I don't think we should push that." She sighed as Bunny's voice grew even more high-pitched. "Yes, if I see him I will mention it to him. I'll check in with you a little later, Bunny." She hung up the phone and took a deep breath.

Being part of the decorating committee meant Samantha was involved in every party that anyone on the committee decided they wanted to host. Bunny's idea to have a memorial for Shayla was a sweet one, but her high-strung nature made it a stressful one. As she stepped back into the kitchen, she noticed how quiet it was. Jo stared at her phone. Eddy stared at Jo.

"I need to run some errands. Do either of you want to join me?" Samantha picked up her purse. "The decorating committee is going to host a memorial for Shayla tomorrow evening."

"Good idea." Jo nodded. "But no thanks, I think I'm going to stay here and wait for Walt."

"Me too." Eddy looked away from Jo long enough to smile at Samantha. "Good luck with Bunny."

"Thanks." Samantha rolled her eyes, adjusted the strap of her purse, then headed for the door. As she walked back to her villa she decided to veer off and check on the activities at Shayla's house. She guessed that Bunny would want to host the memorial near the villa, and she wanted to see if there was a good spot they could use.

As Samantha approached the villa she noticed a CSI van, as well as two police cars, and a few civilian cars. She guessed that Walt was still inside. She started to walk along the path that led up the hill beside the villa, when she saw another car parked in the driveway of the next villa. From the 'For Sale' sign on the front lawn, she knew the villa was still empty. The residents had moved out a few weeks before.

Samantha paused and watched the car. It took a moment, but she recognized it as being the same car that she'd seen that morning when Troy pulled in. Perhaps he'd parked there to stay out of the way of the police. Curious, she walked closer to it. She was almost to the driveway when she realized that there was someone inside of it. She took a sharp breath as Troy looked straight through the windshield at her. She'd been caught. He knew that she'd seen him. She couldn't just walk away now. Would he accuse her of snooping?

Troy stepped out of the car as Samantha lingered beside the driveway.

"Hello there." He nodded to her.

"Hi Troy." Samantha clutched the strap of her purse. "I'm Samantha. I was there this morning, with your mother," she stumbled over her words.

"Yes, I know. I recognized you." Troy leaned back against the side of his car. "I guess you're wondering what I'm doing sitting in my car."

"Not really, no. You don't have to explain yourself to me. I just wanted to say, I'm so sorry for your loss." Samantha offered her hand to him. "I hope that you can find some comfort in what you're able to take with you from her home."

"Comfort?" Troy gave her hand a brief shake as he rolled his eyes. "There's no comfort in sifting through mountains of garbage."

"Well, I'm sure there might be a few things that will benefit you." Samantha settled her hand back at her side, and studied his expression. "This may seem like an impossible task. If you'd like some help, I'd be happy to pitch in."

"No thanks. I'm going to hire someone." Troy ran his hand across his face, then took a breath. "I'm sorry, I don't mean to be rude. It's just all of this happened so suddenly, and I'm not really sure how to handle it. She didn't have her affairs in order, and there are quite a few complications to wade through. When I came here for a visit, I never expected to be faced with all of this."

"I'm sure you didn't. I know that this is a lot for you to take in. We're planning to host a small memorial tomorrow night for your mother. Would you like to join us? Everyone wants to honor your mother."

"Really?" Troy's eyes widened some. "Mother

told me she didn't have any friends here. She didn't know a soul."

"Honestly, I don't know anyone here who knew her. But that doesn't mean we don't want to honor her. I wish I'd had the chance to get to know her. I'm sure she was a wonderful person, and a great mother to you." Samantha looked into his eyes.

"She was a troubled woman." Troy pursed his lips as if he might be holding back a million other things he wanted to say.

"I'm sorry to hear that." Samantha frowned as she met his eyes. "Is there anything you'd like to talk about, or anything I can do for you?"

"Thanks, but I'm fine. My mother and I hadn't been close for a long time. To say this is a shock, is an understatement, but I did know that it would happen eventually." Troy took a breath. "Not like this, of course. Not like this."

"Even when you expect it, loss can shock you. Was she in bad health?" Samantha's heart pounded as she wondered if he might reveal something that could explain what happened. "Did she get herself into some kind of trouble?"

"Her health wasn't perfect, obviously. But her troubles were mostly psychological. She didn't even leave the house enough to create any enemies." Troy rubbed his forehead. "She never would listen to me. I tried to get her to clean up that villa so many times. She even called the police on me for it. I just don't understand what her compulsion was." His hands balled into fists at his sides. "I guess it doesn't matter now. Thanks for your time, Samantha. I'll think about attending the memorial." He gave her a short wave, then walked towards Shayla's villa. Samantha thought about following him, perhaps he would confide more in her. But she decided against it. No matter what happened between Troy and his mother, he was still a grieving son, and though he might not realize how much that would impact him just yet, she didn't want to add stress to his already stressful situation.

alt stepped into his villa to find Jo and Eddy gathered around his kitchen table.

"You'll have to give me a moment, I need to shower and change." Walt wrapped his face mask in a bag, and threw it into the trashcan just outside his back door.

"Can you give us a quick update?" Eddy looked up at him.

"No, sorry. I really can't. I'll just be a minute. Well, technically twenty minutes and thirty seconds. That is the average amount of time that's needed for a thorough shower." He started towards the bathroom, then paused. "Actually, it may be more like twenty-four minutes, as I may need to do some extra scrubbing." He continued down the hall to the shower. As he went over in his mind his time with the detective, he scrubbed every inch of his body. He'd encountered more dust and mold than he'd expected. Although he'd been tempted to run out of the villa in horror, the need to count everything kept him there. He'd helped the detective build a thorough evidence list of everything he could find in the villa, however he still wondered if he might have missed a few things. That wondering would nag at him, he knew it would. Once he was perfectly clean and dressed, he stepped back out into the kitchen. He found that Samantha had joined Jo and Eddy at the table.

"The detective is trying to claim that this was not a robbery." Walt sat down at the table with his three friends. "But he's wrong."

"Yes, he is wrong." Jo looked up from her folded hands that rested on the table. "He's very wrong."

"Wait, why do you say that?" Walt stared at her. "I mean, yes he's wrong, but why do you think he's wrong?"

"Because there was something missing from that villa." Jo took a deep breath, then looked over at Samantha. "I wasn't completely honest with you this morning, Sam."

"What do you mean?" Samantha stared at her.

"When I said I wanted to go with you to deliver the cake, it wasn't to check up on Shayla. It was because I saw something on the television show that I just couldn't believe. An antique vase that is, well, it's practically priceless." Jo sighed and looked down at her hands again. "I know all of you are going to think that I went there to steal it, but I didn't. I just wanted to see if it was real, and not a replica. If it was real, and I could confirm that, I would have told Shayla. She would have been a very rich woman." She shook her head slowly. "I'm sorry for not being completely honest, Sam, but I didn't want you to think poorly of me."

"Jo, I could never think poorly of you." Samantha settled her hand over Jo's, then cleared her throat. "I mean now that I know you. Everything else is in the past."

"Yes, but sometimes the past comes back to haunt you." Jo frowned.

"You keep saying you would have checked to see if it was real." Eddy sat forward in his chair. "Why didn't you?"

"Because when I went through the house, it wasn't there. It certainly wasn't in the spot it had once been, and it wasn't anywhere else that I saw. I had Walt text me a photograph of the evidence list." Jo pulled out her phone. "And it's not on there, either."

"Walt!" Eddy shot a glare in his direction. "That's illegal, you know that, don't you?"

"It was just a little snapshot." Walt straightened up in his chair. "It's a silly thing to be illegal. It's not as if I'm going to give it to the defense attorney, if there ever is a defense attorney, which there will only be if someone figures this out. Besides, I'm the one who built the list, I memorized everything, I just didn't want to have to write it all down."

"Can we just focus on the vase?" Samantha suggested. "It doesn't matter how we know that the vase isn't on the list, what matters is that it isn't."

"And neither is one of the cars from the collection." Walt raised a finger in the air. "Which the detective is also not concerned with. I don't think he really knows what he is doing."

"I wouldn't say that." Eddy shook his head. "I thought he was pretty on top of his game. This kind of investigation is never easy." He turned towards Jo. "So, you went there to steal a vase?"

"No!" Jo jumped up from her chair. "That is not true at all. I would never do that."

"Relax." Eddy held up one hand. "I'm sorry, Jo. It was just a joke. A bad joke."

"A really bad joke." Samantha kicked his foot with hers under the table. "Jo, we all know you weren't there to steal it."

"Thank you." Jo glared at Eddy as she lowered herself back down into her chair. "But the truth is, the vase wasn't there. It's not on the evidence list either. Which means between the time the show was filmed last night, and when Samantha and I went into Shayla's villa this morning, someone took the vase."

"Actually, that makes perfect sense." Walt snapped his fingers. "If it was as valuable as you claim, then someone on the staff of the show probably recognized that. They probably took it."

"With so many things in that villa, Shayla probably wouldn't have even noticed." Eddy shrugged.

"No, you're wrong about that." Walt frowned. "She would have noticed if one single thing was out of place. I'm sure she knew what she had in that villa from top to bottom."

"I'm sure you're right, Walt." Eddy nodded.

"You know, Detective Cooper did mention to me that Troy wanted to get rid of the things in Shayla's villa as soon as possible. I thought maybe it was to hide the evidence, but maybe it was to get his hands on the stuff."

"Maybe Troy thought he was entitled to her stuff." Eddy rubbed his hands together. "Perhaps he thought he could help himself to the vase, and she caught him."

"And he killed his own mother?" Samantha gasped, then gritted her teeth. "What a terrible thought."

"It might be terrible, but if Troy knew how much that vase was worth, it might be possible, too." Jo tapped her fingers on the table. "And when we called the police, only moments after, her estranged husband showed up. I assumed it was just a coincidence at the time, but like Eddy suggested what if he'd been there earlier, then came back to make it look like he hadn't?"

"That would be clever of him." Eddy nodded. "It would throw suspicion off him."

"One thing we know for sure." Walt poked his finger into his palm. "This was a burglary, and a murder. A murderer was in that villa, between nine o'clock last night, and ten o'clock this morning. That's not a huge span of time."

"Isn't there some kind of security camera by the entrance?" Samantha suddenly bolted out of her chair. "They installed them just a few weeks ago. I remember because the decorating committee wanted to throw a party over it, but some people were put off by the idea of it, and called it an invasion of privacy."

"It is an invasion of privacy." Jo narrowed her eyes. "I can't imagine why anyone would want to be constantly recorded."

"If it keeps us more secure, it's fine with me." Eddy gazed back at her. "I mean look at what's happened here. It could have happened to anyone in Sage Gardens. Doesn't that make you worry?"

"I don't worry about things I can't control. And, I fail to see how a camera that reads your license plate will keep you secure. Especially, seeing as cars can use the other exit that doesn't have a camera to leave the property, and people can enter and exit the grounds on foot without being on camera." Jo shrugged.

"Oh, is that what the camera does?" Walt's eyes widened. "It's not just a general camera?"

"No, it automatically focusses on the plate." Jo glanced at her friends as she noticed their interest. "I like to be aware of the changes made around here. I looked into it."

"I bet." Eddy quirked an eyebrow. "Maybe it will lead us to the killer."

"Maybe." Jo studied him. "I have to go."

"Let me walk you out." Walt stood up and escorted her towards the door. "Jo, are you okay?"

"I'm fine, why?" Jo looked back at Eddy.

"Why did you wait so long to tell us about the vase?" Walt looked into her eyes.

"I wanted to be sure. Besides, have you seen the way Eddy has been looking at me all day?" Jo shook her head. "Maybe you and Samantha are ready to let my past be my past, but Eddy never will be."

Nestled in her villa, with all memory of Eddy's prying eyes faded from her mind, Jo stared at her phone. She played the show again on her phone. It felt like she'd watched it a thousand times since the first time she viewed the show. She'd been up most of the night replaying it. Each time, she saw the vase, tucked away on a cluttered shelf. Each time she wondered how it could go missing on the same night that Shayla was killed.

Jo took a deep breath as she watched the

footage again. She wasn't even sure what she was looking for. She glanced over the list of evidence that had been collected from the scene. She couldn't imagine Walt missing anything, but it was possible as the contents of the house seemed endless. However, she hoped to find other things that might be missing. Would someone have broken into the house just to steal the vase? She knew how valuable it was. She also knew that it could be missing for other reasons. But her instincts told her that it had been stolen.

As Jo skimmed through the list again, she looked back at the frozen image on the screen of her tablet. Her eyes widened as she realized that something else was missing. A large photograph with a silver frame. It wasn't just any silver frame, it was old, it looked thick and heavy. It might have been an antique worth quite a bit of money. In the frame was a photograph of a woman who appeared to be Shayla, perhaps fifteen or twenty years younger. She leaned close to a man who had his arm around her. No stretch of Jo's imagination could see this man as Jacob, Shayla's estranged husband. Instead this man was a bit younger than Shayla, with a bright smile, and his hat tipped off to the side as if something playful had just happened. Their faces glowed, whether from the sunny day, or from a romantic encounter, she couldn't be sure. But she doubted that the picture mattered. What mattered was the frame. If it was missing from the evidence list as well, that could mean that whoever took the vase took the frame as well.

Jo sighed as she sat back and wiped at her eyes. It was just after dawn, and she was tired. But she knew she couldn't go to sleep. Not yet. She had to find out who took the vase. While the others tried to piece together who might have wanted to kill Shayla, she wanted to rule out the possibility that Shayla's killer knew absolutely nothing about her, and only wanted the vase. She was aware of several thieves that would be thrilled to get their hands on that vase, and one local fence who they would turn to in order to get it off their hands as quickly as possible. She had something she wanted to do before she followed that lead.

Jo grabbed her purse and headed out through the door. A hush lingered over Sage Gardens. Normally, a few people would already be out, walking, jogging, or at least sitting on their porches. Instead, it was quiet. Still in shock over Shayla's death, most of the community would remain indoors, secretively a bit afraid that what happened to Shayla could happen to them.

Jo decided it was time to face Eddy, and find out exactly why he had that uneasy look on his face when he was near her. She needed to find out before she did anything else. She remembered that look. He'd worn it every time he saw her for the first few months after he had found out about her past. She didn't blame him for it. As a retired cop, of course he would be suspicious of a retired criminal. But she had thought they'd progressed past that point in their friendship. She'd hoped they had.

As Jo reached his villa she wondered if she wasn't just setting herself up for an upsetting experience. Maybe she was better off showing the video to Walt, or to Samantha first. But she knew she couldn't go a minute longer without finding out what was going on in Eddy's mind.

CHAPTER 8

*J*o reached her hand up to knock on the thick wooden door, but before she could it swung open.

"Jo." Eddy stood in the doorway with a bag of trash in one hand. "What are you doing here?"

"Sorry it's so early, Eddy, I need to speak with you about something. Can I come in?" Jo watched his expression for any hint of why he had so much tension around his eyes when he looked into hers.

"Oh sure, of course. Let me just get rid of this." Eddy stepped past her to the trashcan at the top of the driveway. Once he'd deposited the bag, he gestured for her to step into the villa in front of him. "What's on your mind?"

"I'd like to ask you the same question." Jo stepped inside, then turned back to face him.

"I'm sorry? I don't know what you mean?" He pushed the door closed behind him.

"Don't, Eddy. You know you're not a good liar, at least not to me." Jo sighed as she crossed her arms. "I came here to discuss something about the case with you, but I don't want to do that until I find out what your problem is with me."

"My problem?" He stared at her. "You think I have a problem with you?"

"I don't just think it." Jo frowned. "I know it. Please don't play games with me, Eddy. If you've changed your mind about our friendship I can understand, just tell me."

"Stop." Eddy held up his hands and narrowed his eyes. "This is ridiculous."

"It's not." Jo set her jaw. "I know I'm not wrong."

"No, you're not ridiculous. The fact that you can read me so well is what's ridiculous." Eddy took a step closer to her. "Yes, there has been something on my mind about you, but it's not what you think." He smiled. "Jo, I trust you. You know that, don't you?"

"No." Jo shook her head. "I guess I'm not entirely sure of that."

"Well, you should be. The truth is the detective is a bit suspicious of you. He finds it strange that you, being one of the few ex-criminals that live in Sage Gardens, happened to be at Shayla's villa when her body was discovered. He asked me to find out from you, what your whereabouts were in the hours before Shayla died. He didn't think you would be forthcoming to him with the information." He took a deep breath and sighed. "I'm sorry if I've been acting strangely. I've been trying to figure out how to bring this up with you without offending you, without giving you the idea that I might suspect you in any way."

"Ah." Jo rolled her eyes towards the ceiling and shook her head. "Of course, I would be high on the suspect list, I hadn't even considered that."

"You're not high on my suspect list." Eddy met her eyes as she looked back at him. "I hope you know that."

"Thanks." Jo laughed, then sighed. "All right, so what do you plan to tell this detective? It's not as if I had any alibi. I was just at home. That's not going to make him any less suspicious of me."

"Which is why I haven't said a word to him, yet. But he's been texting me, asking me questions. After what you told me yesterday about the vase, I knew I couldn't let you go to the detective with that information. It would only make you look more guilty in his eyes." Eddy frowned. "I'm sorry, I should have been honest with you from the beginning. Honestly, I just wanted to avoid you losing trust in me. You haven't, have you?"

"No Eddy, I haven't." Jo rubbed her hands along her cheeks. "But what are we going to do about this?"

"For now, I can stall him. Then perhaps I can have Walt mention the missing vase to him. At this time, I think you should do your best to avoid speaking to Detective Cooper. I will do my best to protect you from having to." Eddy gave her shoulder a light pat. "Try not to worry too much, Jo."

"Thanks Eddy." She felt a surge of affection for the man who truly had no reason to be fond of her. But he'd turned into one of her best friends. "But that's not the only thing missing from the villa."

"What do you mean?" Eddy led her towards the living room, then settled in his well-worn chair. It creaked as he eased into it.

"This." Jo crouched down beside the chair and pulled out her phone. "I've been watching the television show over and over. I kept hoping to find some clue about the vase. Then I thought, what if it wasn't the only thing taken? I started to replay the video and look for other things that were missing from the evidence list. So far, this is what I've come up with." She paused the show as it showed the silver frame. "The frame isn't on the evidence list, and I doubt it's something that Walt would have missed. It's probably a fairly expensive frame, from the look of it, and it's possibly antique. Nowhere near the value of the vase, but it could be worth quite a bit." She looked up from the phone, to Eddy. "I think it might be missing, too."

"Interesting." Eddy stared at the screen. "Is there any way to make it bigger?"

"Sure." She swiped her fingers across the screen and the image expanded. "Are you trying to look at the people in the picture?"

"I know who that is." Eddy narrowed his eyes as he stared at the picture frame in the video.

"It's Shayla." Jo shrugged.

"Yes, I know it's Shayla." Eddy looked up at her with some exasperation. "But that's not who I'm talking about. I know who the man is in the photograph. I saw him at the police station when I went to speak to the detective about the case. It's Brad.

Her friend that was involved with the murder investigation when they were younger."

"Really?"

"Yes. It sure looks like him." Eddy narrowed his eyes. "I mean, I could be wrong. He does look a bit different now. Time does change us all." He glanced up at her. "Well most of us."

"Thanks Eddy, but now isn't the time for compliments." Jo smiled. "If you're right, and this is the same man, then maybe it has something to do with the investigation."

"Maybe." Eddy ran his hand back through his hair. "So far we have a missing priceless vase, a missing worthless steel car, and a missing picture frame of unknown value. It's an odd combination that's for sure. I'm going to have to update Detective Cooper about all of this."

"Just do me a favor and leave my name out of it?" Jo flashed him a smile.

"Like I said, Jo." Eddy smiled. "I will look out for you. But if it does come to the point that you have to go in for an interview with Detective Cooper, keep in mind that you've done nothing wrong. The system can protect you when you're innocent."

"I hope so." Jo nodded. "I think I'm going to

show this to Walt. He might have seen the frame somewhere in the villa, maybe it just got overlooked."

"You think Walt overlooked something?" Eddy raised an eyebrow.

"Yes, I know it would be a first, but I think it's possible considering how much stuff was crammed in that space. It won't hurt to ask. After that, if you want to report it to Detective Cooper, I fully support that. Let's just get his view on things." Jo started towards the door.

"Jo, wait." Eddy followed her to the door. "We're clear on things, right?" He met her eyes.

"Yes, Eddy." She smiled as she looked back at him. "Thank you. It's nice to know you are someone I can trust."

"Never forget that." He held the door open for her.

As Jo stepped through, she glanced back over her shoulder. "Are you going to come with me?"

"No, I have a few things to follow up on. But let me know what Walt says about the picture frame, okay?" Eddy pulled his phone out of his pocket. "I'll do my best to keep Detective Cooper at bay."

"I will, and thank you." Jo headed down the front walkway away from Eddy's villa. She veered off in the direction of Walt's villa. She hoped that he would be able to give her some insight, or at least some direction as to the next step in their attempt to find out what happened to Shayla. Still exhausted from her long night of watching the recording of the show, she managed to make it to Walt's porch before she gave in to her tired body and sat down in one of his rocking chairs. At the sound of its first creak, the front door opened.

"Jo? What are you doing out and about so early?" Walt stepped up beside her. "Is everything okay? Usually you're in your garden this time of day."

"My garden." Jo nodded. "I need to remember to water it." She covered up a yawn, then looked over at Walt. "I need to show you something."

"What is it?" He leaned close as she showed him the image on her phone.

"Did you see it when you were taking inventory of the items in Shayla's house?" Jo frowned. "I thought maybe somehow it just got overlooked."

"Not a chance." Walt narrowed his eyes. "I would never overlook something that big. It must have gone missing as well."

She explained how Eddy had recognized the man in the picture.

"Interesting." Walt nodded.

"Maybe the frame was worth quite a bit." Jo rocked slowly back and forth in the rocking chair.

"We already know that Troy had been playing games with his mother. He was trying to get rid of her things. Maybe he thought if he just took a little bit at a time she wouldn't notice." Walt paced the length of the porch. "Maybe she caught him in the act."

"Maybe." Jo gazed off into the distance. She noticed a car drive through the gates at the front of Sage Gardens. The sight jogged her memory. "You know, we haven't checked out the footage from the entrance, yet."

"Uh yes, and we won't be able to. Only the police can access something like that." Walt gestured inside. "Why don't you come in? I'll make you some breakfast, and we can talk about the investigation a little more."

"No, I have a better idea." Jo flashed him a grin. "If you're up for it, that is."

"What kind of idea?" Walt's smile faltered. "Why do I get the feeling this is one of those ideas that ends with me in some kind of trouble?"

"Walt, would I ever let anything bad happen to you?" Jo wiggled her eyebrows at him.

"Oh dear." Walt sighed as he gazed at her. "Just what kind of idea do you have?"

"It'll be simple, Walt. All you have to do is distract the guard. I'll slip in, and record the footage with my phone. We can look it over when we get back here." Jo looked into his eyes. "I'll be the only one taking the risk."

"No." He shook his head. "Absolutely not."

"Walt, be reasonable. We need access to that footage. It will at least let us know which cars entered Sage Gardens that night and morning. Why wouldn't we want to know that?" Jo sighed. "Walt, at least think about it."

"I wasn't saying no to the idea. I was saying no to you being the only one to take a risk." He tilted his head towards her. "If you go in, I'm going in with you."

"Walt, that's just too risky." Jo started down the steps of the porch. "It will be much safer if you keep the guard distracted."

"For me." Walt caught her by the elbow as he followed her down the steps. "Jo, I know you don't want to go back to prison. I know that you breaking in there by yourself will put you at risk of that. I'm not going to let you take that risk alone."

"No one is getting arrested." Jo locked her eyes

to his. "Fine, we'll do it together. We can set something up to distract the guard, and while we're inside I'll find the footage and you record it. Got it?"

"Got it." Walt smiled. "That sounds like a far better plan."

"It's not." Jo huffed as she headed down the sidewalk.

"Wait for me!" Walt caught up to her and held back a smile. It was never easy to convince Jo to change her plans. He knew that she only did it for him because she wanted him to feel involved. But he had insisted, because he didn't want her to be alone. She'd told him stories about the years she spent alone as a thief, she'd once even confessed that she sometimes felt more lonely than she imagined was possible. But now, she didn't feel that way anymore. He didn't ever want her to feel that way again.

CHAPTER 9

*W*hen Jo and Walt arrived at the guardhouse, Walt already had an idea in mind for distracting the guard. However, there was no need to. The guardhouse was empty.

"That's strange, isn't it?" Walt frowned as he gazed through the window of the guardhouse.

"It is still fairly early, maybe someone is just late for their shift." Jo shrugged. "I'm going to put my phone out here, near the hedges. If the guard arrives, we'll call the number, and he'll go looking for the phone."

"That's pretty good." Walt nodded. "I had an entire elaborate story about a gator in the lake, but your way sounds better."

"The gator can be our backup plan." Jo winked

at him, then tucked her phone under the hedge. "Hurry, let's get in before the guard arrives." She pulled a bobby pin from her pocket and began to work at the lock on the door. Within only a few seconds she managed to pop it open.

"Amazing." Walt sighed with admiration. "That never gets old."

"Shh." Jo gestured for him to follow her inside.

The guardhouse was small. It was a single room space with several monitors and other equipment lining the walls. There was barely room for the two of them inside, but they managed.

Walt pulled out his phone, as Jo began to tap on the keyboard. He flipped his phone on, but what stared back at him was a blank screen.

"Jo, I don't think my phone is working right." He frowned as he tapped the screen. "I won't be able to record the video with it."

"Oh, we can use mine—" She paused and her eyes widened. "Oh, right we can't, because it's outside."

"Just play it, Jo, I'll be able to remember the plate numbers." Walt tucked his malfunctioning phone into his pocket. Beads of sweat popped up on his forehead, but he ignored them. He knew his excellent memory would be able to retain everything relevant that played on the screen. He just hoped that he would have enough time to watch it.

"Okay, but I don't know how much we can cover before the guard will arrive." Jo glanced towards the door, then hit the play button on the keyboard. As the footage from the night before Shayla's body was found began to play, Jo realized that it might take hours to get through it all. "I'm going to speed it up and just stop it when each car comes through the gate." She glanced at Walt. "Okay?"

"We might miss something." Walt frowned. "Some little detail, that could solve everything."

"That may be true, but we don't have hours to wade through the footage, so we're going to have to speed it up." Jo tapped a key to increase the speed, then froze it when she spotted the first car.

Walt read off the plate of each car that he saw. In the first few hours of the evening there were quite a few. Some of them were likely from the crew of the show. As the night grew later, the cars became sparser. Most residents in Sage Gardens were home by nine, if not a bit earlier. Jo sped up the video until another car came into view.

"That car came and went once already." Walt

narrowed his eyes as he recalled the plate number. "Can we see who is driving it?"

"No, the camera is only positioned to record the license plate, not see into the windows." Jo played the recording again. "Here comes another car, only a little bit later."

"I don't recognize it. At two in the morning? That's pretty late for anyone around here." Walt memorized the plate number. "We'll have to look that one up, too."

"Here it is, only twenty minutes later." Jo paused the video again as the car began to exit.

"Twenty minutes." Walt frowned. "It takes about five minutes to get to Shayla's villa from the front gate. Which would only leave the driver of this car ten minutes to break in, kill Shayla, and hide her body. That's a pretty short time period."

"Yes, it is. But it looks like it's the last car." Jo sped the video up until a police car approached the gate. "Yes, it's the last car to enter and leave before the police arrive. I think there's a good chance that was our killer."

"It's very possible." Walt nodded. "I wish we had the time to watch the entire thing moment by moment. I mean, we have to consider that the killer may not have driven in or out at all. They may have just walked in. There are many places they could have entered the complex on foot."

"That's true." Jo frowned.

"And if the murderer knew about the camera, he probably wouldn't take the risk of being recorded." Walt tapped his chin. "Most of the residents know about the camera, but others may not. It's hidden. If the killer was someone who lived in Sage Gardens, they wouldn't have needed to worry about the camera at all."

"I'd hate to think that it was one of our neighbors." Jo stood up and stretched her hands above her head. "But I know that it's a possibility."

"What's going on here?" The sudden interruption of their conversation, made them both jump.

Jo's fingers passed over the keyboard fast enough to turn the screen back to the current view from the cameras.

Walt stared at the guard as he wondered how much he might know. He couldn't even call Jo's phone to distract him, as his phone wasn't working. He was about to tell the story about the gator in the lake, when Jo stepped forward.

"And just where were you?" Jo scowled at the guard. Her heartbeat quickened in reaction to the arrival of the guard. In seconds, she predicted their future. She and Walt hauled away in hand-cuffs. The man who trusted her, would be faced with great horror the moment that he endured a pat down. She had led him to this moment. She was the reason that he would be subjected to such an inspection. She couldn't let that happen. As she stared at the guard, she hoped that turning the tables on him would help their situation.

"I was out uh, on a call." The guard adjusted his hat. "Someone had some trouble by the community center."

"But aren't you supposed to stay in the guard-house? Isn't there another security guard that walks the grounds?" Jo placed her hands on her hips. "I mean really, when I walked up to the empty guard-house, I had to ask myself, what was the point of investing all of that money into a new camera system."

"The camera records whether I'm here or not." The guard looked over at Walt, but Jo stepped between them.

"You listen to me. The people of Sage Gardens deserve far better than this. They are trusting you to help keep them safe. But instead, let me guess, you were picking up a taco?" Jo gestured to the stain on his shirt. "You should clean that up better, sauce stains."

"Now, that's enough," the guard snapped as he looked between them. "Neither of you are supposed to be in here, and you both know it."

"And we both know that you're not supposed to leave the guardhouse empty, especially soon after someone was murdered." Jo gave him a light pat on the chest. "But this can just be between us. Okay?"

The guard stared hard at each of them, then sighed as he gestured towards the monitors.

"What were you doing?"

"Nothing. Like I said, I wanted to know why the guardhouse was empty. I'm part of the decorating committee." Jo cringed at the very thought. The last group she would ever join, was the decorating committee, however the guard didn't have to know that. "I'll make it quite clear to the committee, and to everyone in Sage Gardens that you weren't at your post. They won't be happy. I believe in second chances. That's why we'll let this go. We'll let this one slide under the rug, just this once."

"Fine!" The guard threw his hands up into the air. "Get out of here, now." He gestured to the door, but before either could reach for it, a car pulled up to the window of the guardhouse. With the three of them huddled together in the small space, they were all visible through the window.

"Detective Cooper." The man tilted his head as he swept his gaze over the three faces. "Walt? What are you doing in there?"

Jo's heart dropped. She was face-to-face with Detective Cooper. Would he recognize her? Would he want to question her right away?

"They were just leaving." The guard grunted, then gestured for them to leave. He also waved the detective through into Sage Gardens.

Jo braced herself as Walt held the door for her. She could talk her way around a guard, but a detective posed a far greater challenge. Jo knew that he was already suspicious of her, catching her in the guardhouse probably didn't lessen that suspicion in any way. But she had no choice as she stepped through the door, she saw the detective pull his car off to the side of the road. Jo had received a few calls and texts from him that she had ignored. She presumed that he was trying to contact her because Eddy hadn't got back to him in relation to her. In her mind, there was only one reason for the detective to try to contact her. She glanced over at Walt.

"Let's go this way." Walt tipped his head in the opposite direction of their villas. It was also the opposite direction of the detective who had just stepped out of the car.

"Yes, let's do that." Jo started towards the sidewalk. When she felt Walt's arm snake through hers, she shot him a brief look of gratitude. That gratitude faded as the detective waved to them.

"Walt! I need to speak with you."

Walt gave her arm a light pat.

"You go on ahead without me, I'll check in with you later."

"Thanks Walt." Jo pulled away from him, and hurried down the sidewalk.

"Wait a minute!" The detective's sharp tone cut through Jo. Her feet ached to run, but she rooted them to the ground. A fleeing suspect could easily turn into a dead suspect, that was something that she already knew. "Jo, right?" He trotted up behind her, with Walt at his side.

"Oh, Jo has an appointment to get to, she's in a bit of a hurry." Walt managed to get between them. "Is there something that I can help you with, Detective?"

"I'm sure she can spare just a minute." Detective Cooper slid his hands into his pockets as he swept his gaze over Jo. "I have been calling, I've left many messages. Didn't you get them, Jo?"

"Sorry Detective, I've been very busy." Jo took a breath as she did her best to meet his eyes. Looking away would indicate guilt. She'd learned that, too. She just needed to present a confident, relaxed image. If she could do that, he hopefully wouldn't be the least bit interested in her. "What did you need?"

"I need to speak with you." Detective Cooper's jaw clenched for a moment, then relaxed, as he gazed at her. "You've been quite hard to track down."

"I'm right here." Jo shrugged as she smiled. "Not too hard to find."

"So you say." He raised an eyebrow. "So, you're a friend of Walt's?"

"A good friend." Walt volunteered.

"Great." He nodded, then stepped closer to Jo. "Maybe, you and I could go somewhere, and talk? Perhaps, a cup of coffee at the diner?"

"Like I said, I'm fairly busy." Jo's heart skipped a beat. No, she didn't want to go anywhere with the detective. When he put two and two together she knew that he would want to take her down to the station.

"Listen Jo, I don't mean to frighten you, but I do need to speak with you. Either we can share a cup of coffee, or I can give you a ride down to the station."

"How is that not supposed to frighten her?" Walt's shoulders straightened as he glared at the detective. "How dare you —"

"It's okay, Walt." Jo couldn't help but smile a little as he jumped to her defense. "Coffee sounds a lot better than a police station."

"Then I'll go with you." Walt slid his arm around her shoulders.

"I'll be fine." Jo gave him a light kiss on his cheek. "I'm sure the detective won't bite. Will you, Detective Cooper?"

"No, I won't bite." He smiled as he looked between them. "Don't worry, Walt, she'll be in very good hands."

"Good indeed." Walt cut his eyes towards the detective. "If she says she had nothing to do with this, then she had nothing to do with this."

"I'm not accusing anyone." The detective raised his hands in the air. "All I did was invite someone for coffee."

"Fine. One coffee." Jo nodded. "I'll meet you there."

"We could just ride together." Detective Cooper gestured to his nearby car.

"No thanks, I'll meet you there." Jo brushed her hair back over her shoulders and held his gaze. Inwardly, she dared him to challenge her decision. Maybe his car was unmarked, but it was still a police car, and she had no intention of getting into it.

"Jo." Detective Cooper stepped in front of her before she could get too far from him. "Are you actually going to meet me there? Or should I expect to be drinking my coffee alone?"

"I'll be there." Jo looked straight into his eyes. "I have no reason not to be."

"Great." The detective nodded to her, then to Walt, before he turned back to his car.

"Jo, are you sure you don't want me to come with you?" Walt met her eyes.

"No, I'll be fine." She took a deep breath. "If I need you, I'll call you, Walt."

CHAPTER 10

*E*ddy looked up at the sound of a knock on his front door. It jolted him from the contemplative space he'd settled into. Shayla, a recluse, didn't do anything to harm anyone. How did she end up dead? When he opened the door, Walt hurried inside.

"I have some plate numbers. Do you think your friend at the police station could run them for us?"

"Chris?" Eddy nodded as he looked over the list that Walt handed him. "I'm sure he'd be willing to run them through for us." He looked back up at him. "How did you get these?"

"I might have seen the security video from the front entrance of the retirement community." Walt cleared his throat. "Which brings me to another point that I feel I should share with you."

"Please do." Eddy raised his eyebrows as he stared at him and sat back down in a chair at the kitchen table. "It seems there's a lot you might need to tell me."

"Jo and I encountered Detective Cooper this morning. He insisted on speaking with her." Walt ran his hand along the back of his neck. "I'm not sure that the meeting will go well."

"Did he take her down to the station?" Eddy jumped up from his chair.

"Wait." Walt stepped in front of him. "As far as I know they were going to have coffee at the diner. If anything about that changed, Jo promised to call me."

"I don't understand, how did you encounter Detective Cooper in the first place?" Eddy frowned as he eased back down into his chair. The last thing he wanted was for Jo to be alone with the detective. "Why didn't you go with her?"

"She insisted that she meet with him alone. You know how determined Jo can be." Walt wrung his hands. "But maybe I should have insisted that I go with her. I'm never sure what to do in these types of situations." He sat down in an empty chair, across from Eddy. "We went to the guardhouse this morning, to see if we could view the footage. When we were about to leave, Detective Cooper pulled in. He spotted us, then pulled over and insisted on speaking to us."

"I see." Eddy folded his hands on the table, then took a deep breath. "Okay, if he took her to the diner there's less chance that he's planning to take her in for questioning. But depending on what Jo says at that meeting, it could end up that way."

"What Jo says, at what meeting?" Samantha stepped in and dropped her purse on the couch in the living room before continuing into the kitchen. "Where is Jo?"

As Eddy filled her in, Samantha's lips tightened more with every word.

"Excuse me." She marched back through the living room, snatched up her purse, then slammed the door closed behind her.

"Where do you think she's going?" Walt stared after her.

"I believe she's going to insist that Jo not be interrogated." Eddy sighed and rubbed his palm along his forehead. "I would not want to be Detective Cooper right now."

"Maybe we should go, too?" Walt started to stand up.

"No, I think we'd better find out what we can on these plate numbers. The sooner we can come up with some concrete evidence, the better chance there is that Detective Cooper will leave Jo alone." Eddy pulled out his cell phone. "Let me call Chris and see what he can do for us." He stepped into his bedroom and called his friend's number. Chris was a tech at the police station. Eddy had taken him under his wing when he first started out, and as a result Chris did small favors for him when asked. But this wasn't the smallest of favors.

"Hi Chris." Eddy coaxed his voice into being cheerful. "How are you doing today?"

"You want something." Chris chuckled. "You're never that friendly unless you want something."

"I have friendly moments." Eddy frowned.

"Not with me you don't." Chris laughed again. "Just tell me what you need."

"I just need a few plate numbers run through. Do you think you could help me with that?" Eddy peered at the list in his hand.

"I guess, but make it quick, things are a little tense around here." He lowered his voice. "Detective Cooper is closing in on a suspect."

"He is?" Eddy's muscles tensed. Was it Jo?

"Yes, he's being pretty tight-lipped about the whole thing, but the rumor is that he might even make an arrest today." Chris cleared his throat. "But you didn't hear that from me. So, what are the plate numbers?"

Eddy fed him each plate number as his head swam with the possibility that Jo could be in danger. Was she already in handcuffs?

"All right, this could take a little while. I'll text you with the results."

"What about the cause of death?" Eddy narrowed his eyes. "Did they figure it out, yet?"

"Right now, they're calling it suffocation, but they haven't finished the exam yet."

"Suffocation." Eddy pursed his lips. "Thanks Chris." He hung up the phone before his friend could say another word. "Okay, Chris is running the plates for us right now." Eddy gazed at Walt and wondered if he should tell him the rest. He decided against it. If Jo was being arrested, there was nothing they could do to stop it, and Walt would insist on trying to get in the middle of it. Which could only make things worse. Knowing that Shayla was suffocated, didn't add anything to their current investigation, and he knew that Walt would fixate on the details, which wouldn't be good for him, or the case.

"There's something else that I want to look into, though." Eddy sat back down at the table and set his phone between them. "Troy." He pointed to the picture of the young man on his phone. "It turns out Shayla called the police on him several times. I found out by perusing the police reports for Shayla's address. I also checked previous addresses."

"Did I hear that correctly?" Walt's eyes widened as he stared down at the picture. "His own mother called the police on him?"

"Yes. From what I understand, each time it was because Troy had attempted to remove items from Shayla's villa. He claimed it was to help her get things cleaned up for her health and safety, and I assumed that was the case at first. But now." Eddy frowned. "The vase, the car, the picture frame are all missing. What if Troy took them?"

"On the show, Shayla did mention that she bought the first car in the collection for Troy. He might have felt he owned it. But why the vase and the picture frame?" Walt shook his head. "That doesn't make sense to me."

"Because you're assuming that Troy didn't have criminal intent." Eddy narrowed his eyes as he rested his hands on the table. "But perhaps he wasn't motivated by frustration with his mother, or revenge over some form of neglect in his childhood. Maybe, he was motivated by one of the classic causes of murder. Greed."

"You mean he just wanted to sell her valuable items?" Walt nodded. "That would make sense, especially if he had some kind of financial difficulty. Can you get me his financial records?"

"I already have. I arranged for one of my police contacts to get them for all the main suspects yesterday, and they came through just before." Eddy took out his phone and tapped a few keys as he muttered. Technology frustrated him. "I'll send them to you now."

"Troy's records are a good place to start while we're waiting on information from the plates to come in."

Jo pulled open the door to the diner. The thick glass door seemed heavier than usual. She gave it a hard tug to pull it shut. As she took a few steps into the mostly empty diner, she caught sight of the detective at a small table in the back. Her breath caught in her throat in the same moment that her heart began to race. How could she have agreed to this? She closed her eyes, took a slow breath, and reminded herself that sweat indicated guilt. If she acted nervous, his suspicion would only grow. She glanced at the few customers at other tables and hoped that their breakfasts wouldn't be ruined by what was about to unfold.

"Jo." Detective Cooper smiled as he stood up from the table. "I ordered us both some coffee."

"Thanks." Jo pulled out the other chair at the table and sat down in it. She did her best to look straight into his eyes. Evasiveness stokes suspicion, she reminded herself. It had been some time since she'd had to play the part of an innocent person. She had no idea if she was still good at it.

"I appreciate you meeting with me." Detective Cooper flipped open his notebook on the table in front of him. As he trailed his fingertips along the neat writing, he mouthed a few words, then nodded. "Yes, so let's start from the beginning."

"The beginning?" Jo's stomach twisted. Did he want to know about her entire life of crime?

"When you and Samantha met up that morning, to bring the cake to Shayla." The detective retrieved a pen from the inside pocket of his suit jacket and tapped it lightly on the notebook. "I just want to make sure I didn't miss anything."

"Samantha wanted to make sure that everything was okay with Shayla. We watched the television show the night before, and Shayla looked very upset as the show ended." Jo smiled some. "Samantha is very kind that way. She always likes to make sure that everyone is okay."

"That's a wonderful way to be." Detective Cooper nodded, glanced down at his notebook, then back up to her. "But that's not why you went there, is it?"

"I went with her." Jo shrugged as her chest began to tighten. "Just to keep her company."

"See Jo, I do know that people change." He lowered his voice in the same moment that he leaned closer to her. "We all have our pasts. But when you lie to me, that makes me wonder, has she really changed, or is she just trying to con me?"

Jo stared into his eyes. He appeared to be able to read her quite easily. Or was it just a bluff to get her to admit to things that she didn't want to admit? With only seconds to make a decision, she took the easiest path, honesty.

"I wanted to go with her because I was curious about something." Jo looked up as a waitress walked up to their table. Once the drinks had been settled, and the waitress moved on to another table, Jo turned her attention back to the detective.

"The vase, right?" The detective set his phone on the table next to his notebook, tapped a few keys, then turned the phone to face her. "This one?"

Jo clenched her teeth as she wondered just how much Eddy had told the detective. Clearly, he knew about the items missing from the house now.

"Yes." Jo toyed with the mug in front of her, but didn't dare to take a sip.

"You recognized it as a valuable item, didn't you?" Detective Cooper slid the phone closer to her. "Just how much is it worth?"

"I didn't take it." Jo's heartbeat quickened, which made breathing difficult. "I know that's what you must think, but I didn't take it."

"No, of course not. You just wanted to go see it. You were just curious." Detective Cooper lifted one eyebrow. "No harm in that."

"You're mocking me, aren't you?" Jo narrowed her eyes as she looked at him. "You can do that all you want, but I didn't take the vase. It wasn't there when we arrived."

"You mean when you broke into Shayla's

house?" The detective's tone hardened, as did his eyes. His coffee mug sat untouched as well.

"I didn't break in." Jo licked her lips and wondered if tossing hot coffee at him would be an effective means of escape. No, Jo don't even think about it. Her mind filled with the years she'd spend in prison for assault on a police officer, and she really didn't want to hurt him.

"The door was open, but you didn't have permission to enter." Detective Cooper tipped his head to the side. "Isn't that true?"

"Samantha was worried." Jo felt sweat begin to gather on her forehead. "We both were. We just wanted to make sure that she was okay."

"And you wanted to look for that vase." Detective Cooper tapped the pen on his notebook again. "The one that you didn't take. The one that you didn't break into Shayla's house to find."

The pounding of the pen against the paper sounded far louder due to the panic in Jo's mind. The diner had been a trick. He knew he would never get her down to the station willingly, so he'd brought her here. But she wouldn't be getting out of the diner without handcuffs around her wrists. Her hands flexed in reaction to the thought.

CHAPTER 11

"*E*xcuse me!" Samantha's sharp voice cracked through the otherwise quiet diner as she marched in the direction of the table where Jo and Detective Cooper sat. "You have no right to interview this woman without her lawyer present." Samantha placed both of her hands on the top of the small table, between Jo and Detective Cooper. "This harassment ends now."

"Samantha, you need to calm down." Detective Cooper stood up, his eyes narrowed, and his voice low.

"I will not calm down. Jo does not have a lawyer present. You are questioning her about a crime, and she needs to have representation." Samantha gestured for Jo to stand up as she stared at the detective. "Please take your seat, we're leaving."

"Not yet, you're not." Detective Cooper stepped around the side of the table and caught Jo by the arm just before she could turn towards the front door. "I have some more questions for you."

"Sorry, you'll have to write them down and mail them to her. Or wait so she can get proper representation." Samantha grabbed Jo's other wrist and gave it a tug.

Jo did her best to remain calm, but as she was pulled between the detective and her friend, she became aware that things were going to get ugly quickly.

"Samantha's right." Jo brushed the detective's hand off her wrist. "I shouldn't be speaking with you without a lawyer present."

"So, now you need a lawyer?" Detective Cooper stared into her eyes. "Personally, I think it makes someone look like they have something they need to hide, if they need a lawyer to help them through it."

"You can say what you want, Detective, but I have not committed any crime here, and I'm leaving." Jo spun on her heel, and with Samantha at her side, she headed for the door. With each step she took, she expected the detective to chase after her, but she reached the front entrance of the diner, and paused beside the steps. "Thanks Sam." Jo looked over at her friend with a warm smile. "I don't know what I was thinking. I never should have agreed to have a coffee with him."

"You were thinking that he might be a good guy that could help you out. No need to apologize for that." Samantha slung her arm around her shoulders.

"It's no use. I can't concentrate." Walt pushed his computer aside and closed his eyes. "I'm sorry, Eddy. All I can think about is Jo and that detective. Logically, he should arrest her."

"We don't know that for sure." Eddy frowned.

"I do. I've run through all of the scenarios in my mind, and if I was the detective I would feel compelled to arrest and interrogate Jo." Walt sighed and stood up from the table.

"Good thing you're not the detective." Eddy glowered at him as he stood up from the table as well. "Police work isn't just about evidence and law, it's about instinct."

"And what do you think Detective Cooper's

instincts are going to tell him about a former cat burglar who happened to discover the body of a murder victim that had been robbed?" Walt shook his head as his stomach churned. He hated to feel uneasy. He carefully aligned everything in his life to prevent the feeling of unease. Yet, here he was. "I have to go see what's happening at the diner." He started towards the door.

"I'm right behind you." Eddy grabbed his keys.

Within minutes they were at the diner. Walt spotted Samantha and Jo on the top of the steps outside the front door of the diner. Relief flooded through him. She wasn't in handcuffs. She wasn't being hauled away. His heart lurched at the thought. What could he do to save her if that happened? In the past his logical mind would have prevented him from taking any chances, but now, he knew he would do just about anything to protect Jo.

"Ladies." Walt looked up at them from the bottom of the steps. "I guess we missed the fireworks?"

"What are you two doing here?" Jo descended the steps of the diner and locked eyes with Walt, then looked over at Eddy.

"Had to make sure that you didn't get carted off." Eddy winked at her.

"We just wanted to make sure that everything went smoothly." Walt offered her his hand as she descended the last step.

"Thanks." Jo took his hand, but released it as she reached the sidewalk.

Walt let his hand fall back to his side as he studied her. "Did it go well?"

"Well? Define well." Jo frowned. "He thinks I broke into Shayla's villa to steal the vase. He didn't mention anything about murder, but I'm sure that was coming up next. Thankfully, Samantha charged in before he could get that far." She looked over at Samantha, whose cheeks were still flushed. "Thank you, again."

"I can't believe it worked, honestly." Samantha paused beside Eddy. "I thought he might just end up arresting me instead."

"Listen, no one is getting arrested." Eddy held up his hands and offered a calm smile. "Keep in mind, none of us are guilty of anything. If we get distracted by worrying about the detective digging into us, then we're never going to get this solved."

"That's easy for you to say, Eddy." Jo sighed and rested her hands on her hips. "You're not the one he's digging into."

"I'm also not the one who found the body." Eddy

hesitated, his eyes widened, and his voice softened. "I'm also not the one who broke into Shayla's house."

"All right fine, we made a bad decision." Samantha shook her head as she fell into step beside her friends and walked with them into the parking lot. "But if we hadn't, Shayla might still be in that closet. Who knows how long it would have been until she was discovered."

"Her son was active in her life." Jo shrugged. "He might have checked on her."

"Unless he's the one who put her in there in the first place." Eddy paused beside his car. "We have reason to believe he might have been interested in stealing the car, the vase, and the frame. We believe he might have had a history of trying to steal from his mother. Maybe, she'd had enough this time, or maybe he'd had enough of her calling the cops on him. Either way, something might have gone wrong this time."

"You think he was stealing from her?" Samantha's eyes widened. "I mean, I just assumed that he really was trying to get things cleaned up."

"It's easy to assume that. But it didn't appear as if he went about it in a very supportive way. It's possible that he might have a habit he needs to supply, if you know what I mean." Eddy gave the length of his finger a sharp sniff.

"Now, he's a drug addict?" Walt sighed. "We have no idea if any of this is true, Eddy."

"No, we don't, but we can follow the lead and find out." Eddy leaned back against his car. "Until Chris gets back to us with the information from the plates, which by the way—" He paused and looked over at Jo. "If you're interested in staying out of handcuffs, breaking into a guardhouse is probably not the best idea."

"I know, I know." Jo rolled her eyes. "But we got the information, didn't we?"

"Indeed, we did." Walt flashed her a smile.

"As I was saying, this is the best lead we have for the moment." Eddy frowned.

"Actually, I have one more lead I can follow." Jo gave the three of them a brief wave. "I'll meet up with you later."

"Jo, wait." Walt jogged after her. "Where are you going?"

"Somewhere that you can't." She winked at him, then pulled open her car door.

"Then I'm definitely going with you." He walked around to the passenger side.

"No, you're definitely not." Jo crossed her arms as she stared across the top of the car at him.

"Why not?" Walt frowned as he fought against a few illogical emotions that raced through him. "Isn't it always safer to use the buddy system? If there are two of us, that lessens the risk."

"Not in this case. When dealing with certain people, it's always better to go alone." Jo started to get into the car, but paused when Walt lingered on the passenger side. "Walt, seriously."

"I know that you are serious about this, Jo, but so am I. I'm going with you." He pulled open the passenger side door.

"Walt!" Jo frowned, glanced over her shoulder in the direction of their friends, then turned her attention back to him. "I need you to let this go. I know what I'm doing."

"I know what you're doing, too." Walt narrowed his eyes. "That's why I'm going with you. You're going to take risks that you shouldn't, and you might get yourself tangled up in something that you shouldn't. I'm going to be there to make sure that doesn't happen."

"Walt, I don't have time for this." Jo glared across the top of the car at him. "You need to step aside."

"Do I?" Walt locked his eyes to hers, then slid into the passenger seat, and pulled the door closed behind him. His heart pounded. He wasn't one to make a stand, but he had no plans to back down. He knew how stubborn Jo could be, and he planned to be just as stubborn.

"Walt?" Jo poked her head in through the driver's side door. "This is foolish."

"It's foolish to do something like this on your own." Walt stared straight ahead through the windshield. "Like it or not, Jo, you have people that care about you, now. So, are we going?" He glanced at his watch. "The later it gets the more likely an arrest warrant is being ordered for you."

"Ugh." Jo sighed, stared at him a moment longer, then slid into the driver's seat. "Fine, you can come along for the ride." She started the car.

Walt glanced over at her. He reached out, gave her hand a light pat, then rummaged in his pocket for some sanitizing wipes. As he began to wipe down the interior, Jo cranked up the radio, and gunned the engine.

"Do you think they'll be okay?" Eddy stared after Jo and Walt.

"Yes, they'll be fine." Samantha winked at him, then leaned back against his car. "So, you came to play hero, huh?"

"You beat me to it." Eddy looked over at her as a slow smile spread across his lips. "Do I want to know what you said to Detective Cooper?"

"Do you?" Samantha grinned. "Probably not."

"Great." Eddy sighed and laughed at the same time. "You know I'm trying to create a good relationship with the man."

"You do it your way, I'll do it mine." Samantha gave him a light pat on the arm. "Shall we go back to my place and have a good look into Troy's history? Maybe we can find something solid to prove that he's involved in these thefts. We're going to need something to turn the attention away from Jo."

"Detective Cooper is a reasonable man. I'm sure she's not his top suspect." Eddy's cheeks flushed.

"You're sure?" Samantha shook her head, then stared into his eyes. "I'm sure you're lying."

"I'll meet you at your place." Eddy stood up from the car. "We have a lot to talk about."

"See you there." Samantha gazed at him a moment longer in an attempt to figure out exactly what his last words meant. Was he referring to the case, or her rogue attempt to protect Jo? With Eddy's history in law enforcement, she knew he could get a little touchy when she fought against it. But her history with law enforcement led her to a rather jaded view of some police officers. Eddy had proven himself to be a reasonable and reliable person, but that didn't mean that everyone who wore a badge was.

On the drive to her villa, Samantha considered the possibility that she might have overplayed her hand with the detective. Eddy was right, they didn't want him to be their enemy. She certainly didn't want to make him any more suspicious of their motive for being at Shayla's villa. She pulled into her driveway, and caught sight of Eddy's car in her rearview mirror. She would find out soon enough what he wanted to talk about.

Samantha stepped out of the car and waited for Eddy to join her. Despite her expectations that he would have a lot to say, he remained silent. She unlocked the door and headed for the kitchen to make them both some coffee.

"How about some music to get our minds

moving?" Samantha turned on her CD player as she walked past it.

"That might help." Eddy nodded as he settled at the kitchen table. "Thanks for the coffee." He smiled as she set a mug down in front of him.

"What do we already know about Troy?" Samantha sat down across from Eddy and relaxed as the music began to drift through her senses. "If we can get to a jumping off point then I might be able to dig up some more information about him."

"We know that Shayla alleged that he stole from her, repeatedly. Walt was able to pull some evidence of financial trouble in the past, but currently his finances look fairly stable. Maybe he just wanted more?" Eddy put his feet up on one of the empty chairs. "We know that he was frustrated with Shayla's behavior for some time before she was killed. Which means that he had time to build up anger, and resentment. He had the opportunity to kill her, that's for sure."

"But that's what makes it less believable. He had plenty of opportunity to do it. Why would he choose now?" Samantha frowned as she began to type on her computer. "With all of the attention from the television show, it wouldn't be the best time to make a move like that."

"Maybe, but murders don't always happen at the best time. Most of the time they happen when someone snaps. Maybe he just couldn't take it anymore." Eddy sighed. "However, suffocation is not usually how someone snaps."

"Suffocation?" Samantha looked up at him. "You found out the cause of death?"

"Yes. Chris told me when I called about the plate numbers that Jo and Walt collected. I should be hearing back from him fairly soon on those." Eddy tapped the back of her computer. "Work your magic. We need to rule Troy in or out once and for all. I still say that the estranged husband is a good suspect. He was there when you found Shayla's body. That is too much of a coincidence for me."

"That may be true. I'll look into both of them." Samantha cringed. "I hate to think of Troy possibly killing his own mother. But the way he spoke about her, it did sound as if he harbored quite a bit of resentment."

"Family can make the worst enemies." Eddy shuddered. "While you're doing that, I'll check in with Chris to see if there's an update on the plates." He stood up from the table.

"Sounds good." Samantha began a search for Troy. As an investigative journalist she'd learned a lot about digging into people's lives. Social media made it a lot easier. But not everyone was active on social media. As it turned out, Troy was. Very active. As she sorted through multiple accounts, all filled with pictures and posts, she wondered how he ever had time to get anything else done. She heard the front door shut as Eddy stepped out to make his call. As she skimmed over one of Troy's rants, she noticed something interesting about it. He spoke about his frustration with people not trying to improve themselves, accused most people of being stuck in their ways and refusing to get help even when it was self-destructive. It all seemed to relate to his situation with his mother.

Samantha shifted gears and began to look into Jacob. It didn't take long for her to find that he had some issues. His credit score was extremely low, and he had a few evictions on his record.

"Where do you live, Jacob?" Samantha tried a few different ways to find a current address for him, but none turned out to be accurate. Then she stumbled across a social profile that had him listed as a boyfriend. The woman who listed him appeared to be quite a bit younger than him. Her posts were full of luxurious images, including snapshots of a large house. In one photograph she and Jacob stood hand-in-hand in front of the house.

"Aha." Samantha smiled. "Now I know where to find you, Jacob. Looks like you are moving up in the world."

Samantha jotted down the address of the house, along with the phone number of Nina Best, the woman he stood beside. She obviously had her finances together. Maybe Jacob wanted to ensure his wealth. Maybe he wanted to marry Nina, and Shayla refused to give him a divorce. Her eyes suddenly widened. "Oh, tell me it's not true!"

Samantha picked up her phone and called Jeremy, an old contact that could hopefully get her the information she needed. He was a financial reporter and had many contacts in the insurance industry that could access records. They owed each other so many favors that they had lost track. Minutes later, Jeremy called back and confirmed her suspicions. Jacob had a life insurance policy on Shayla. Since they were still married, he was still the beneficiary.

Samantha's lips tightened as she put the pieces together.

"A new life, a new wife, and a nice little nest egg. That's pretty good motive, Jacob."

CHAPTER 12

*E*ddy stood on the front porch and waited for Chris to pick up. After several rings he guessed that Chris might not answer. That wasn't like him. Even when he was in the middle of important work, he would usually answer the phone. For a second, he wondered if he'd asked for one too many favors. Then the line picked up.

"Eddy, sorry I haven't gotten back to you."

"No problem, what's going on?" Eddy leaned against the pillar of the porch.

"It's a little crazy here. I've got some information for you." Chris' voice dropped. "But none of this can come back to me, all right, Eddy?"

"Yes, I'll be careful, Chris. I promise." He

frowned as he heard the strain in Chris' voice. "Why? Is something going on?"

"Detective Cooper runs a very tight ship, and if he finds out that I've been leaking information, he's not going to be pleased. He came back in today from meeting with someone and he was livid. I've never seen him so worked up. He let us all know what our jobs were, and that we needed to do them better." Chris sighed. "I'm not sure what to think of this guy now. Maybe he's just power hungry. I thought he was in it for good reasons, but the way he spoke to us today, I think he might just like bossing people around."

"Try not to be too hard on him. Working a murder can be very stressful." Eddy felt a pang of guilt as he realized he knew exactly why Detective Cooper had returned to the station in such an angry manner. He'd been on the receiving end of Samantha's anger, and it wasn't easy to endure. "What about the information?"

"I'm going to send it to you. I cross-checked the details with residents in Sage Gardens and the crew from the show. From what I can tell there are three plates that don't belong to residents or crew members. I'll send you all the info, but the three plate numbers are going to be on Detective Cooper's radar as well. He must have looked at the footage recently as he also asked me to search the plates. I just hope he doesn't know I gave you the information." He sighed nervously.

"He won't, I'll never tell him." Eddy began to pace the length of the porch.

"Hopefully, this cracks the case. Good luck, Eddy."

"Thanks, Chris." Eddy hung up the phone, then waited as Chris sent through an email with a link to the information on each plate. As he walked back into the kitchen, he found Samantha bent over her computer. It would be easy to be upset with her about the way she spoke to Detective Cooper, but he couldn't be. She was an intelligent, fiery woman, whose determination was unshakable. She'd never let anything intimidate her, and she called out injustice wherever she saw it. Maybe, she was a little out of hand that morning, but she had her reasons.

"I've got some information on the plates." Eddy sat down across from her.

"Oh good, I've got some information about Jacob, too. Did any of the plates belong to him?" Samantha turned her attention to Eddy.

"Yes, take a look." He slid the information across his screen. "The first car that went through the entrance belongs to Troy. The second one belongs to a woman named Gina Post." He stared at her picture for a moment, then shifted to the last text. "The third one belongs to the ex-husband." He smiled as he tapped a finger against the table. "I told you, the ex-husband did it. Why else would he be going into Sage Gardens after midnight?"

"Well, wait a minute." Samantha held up her hand before he could speak. "No, I don't disagree with you. But consider this, Troy's car went through there, too. It was the first one. If his father came through later, wouldn't he have interrupted the murder?" Samantha leaned across the table and spoke in a quieter tone. "What if they worked together on this, Eddy? Troy went in first, and his father showed up a little bit later? It can't be a coincidence, can it? Troy must have called Jacob, why else would he have randomly shown up?"

"I hadn't even thought of that." Eddy pressed his fingertips against his forehead. "I guess it's possible, but why would they take separate cars if they planned to attack her together?"

"Maybe they thought it would look less suspicious?" Samantha turned the computer towards Eddy. "I found something interesting about Troy. He is the leader of a support group for children of hoarders. It's pretty clear to me that he had a problem with his mother. From one of his recommendations, I also found that he's been seeing a psychologist himself, so I think he's had a hard time dealing with his childhood, and ongoing relationship with his mother."

"Interesting. That may mean he's a little unstable, or it may just mean he has issues to work through like most of us. But what about his father?" Eddy raised an eyebrow. "Did he post anything about him? Was he connected with him?"

"Actually, no. I didn't see a single post about his father. But I did find quite a bit of interesting information about Jacob." Samantha slid her notepad towards him. "He's about to become a very rich man, thanks to the life insurance policy that he is still the beneficiary of, and thanks to his wife's murder."

"Really?" Eddy's eyes widened as he looked down at the information. "Detective Cooper must know about this, which means he has a better suspect than Jo."

"Yes, and that's a good thing. I'm also curious about this woman he's living with, Nina Best." She turned to face her computer.

"Don't worry about it now. Let's focus on Gina

Post. We need to clear that car from being related to the crime." Eddy sat back down at the table.

"Gina Post? But why? She's not a suspect." Samantha looked over the top of the computer at him.

"For the moment she isn't. We have no idea who she is, or why she entered Sage Gardens at that time of night. These are the things that we need to find out. Maybe she was just someone out driving in the middle of the night. Chris cross-checked the list with residents at Sage Gardens and the crew from the show, maybe he missed her. But I don't know any Gina Post in Sage Gardens. Do you?"

"No." Samantha's eyes widened. "Until recently I'd say I knew everyone in Sage Gardens. But I didn't know Shayla. So, it's possible she's a resident here. If she's not, what would she be doing driving into Sage Gardens at that hour?"

"Exactly." Eddy smiled. "While you work on that, I'm going to make a few calls. I think I can find out a bit more about Troy's father."

"Sounds good." Samantha focused in on the computer again.

Eddy sat back in his chair and watched her for a moment. She could find information on just about anyone. If he'd known her when he was still wearing a badge, she would have been an invaluable resource.

"Good job on finding out about the life insurance, Sam."

"Hmm?" Samantha glanced up and nodded. "Thanks, busy now." She turned her attention back to the computer.

Eddy smiled to himself, then picked up his phone again. Maybe, he and Samantha didn't always agree, but he was glad they were on the same side.

"Where are we going?" Walt looked over at Jo, as she turned down a long, deserted road.

"I don't have to answer any questions." Jo slowed the car down.

"No, but it would be nice to know why we're driving out into the middle of nowhere." Walt took a deep breath.

"I know, it's hard for you not to know what to expect, which is why I told you not to come." Jo shot him a brief glare. It was hard for her to stay focused on the task at hand with him beside her.

"Okay fine." Walt frowned, folded his hands in

his lap, and stared straight forward.

Jo detected the tension in his posture and knew that his valiant attempt to bottle up his anxiety wouldn't last very long.

"We're almost there. Does that help?" Jo spared him a quick smile.

"Yes." Walt exhaled.

Jo turned down another road, which led to only one building. She parked a good distance from the door.

"We're here."

"Okay." Walt surveyed the building. "And?"

Jo swept her long, dark hair up into a tight ponytail, then looked over at him.

"And you stay in the car." Jo stepped out and started to close her car door. She heard Walt's snap shut before she could. "Walt!" She looked across the top of the car at him. "This is not the kind of place where you want to be."

"If it's where you are, it's where I want to be." He locked his eyes to hers. "Are we going to stand out here and argue, or are we going to go in and find out some information?"

"Walt." Jo sighed and slammed her door shut. "This is not a game."

"I know." Walt walked around the front of the

car, to her side. "Which is why I'm here. Just in case you need backup."

"I won't need it." Jo stepped around him and headed for the warehouse. A quick glance over her shoulder revealed Walt had quickened his pace to catch up with her. She set her jaw and did her best to summon patience instead of fury. She knew that Walt meant well, but that didn't make it any safer for him to participate in this mission with her. "All right fine. But if you're coming with me, no talking. And no pointing out health hazards. Got it?" She met his eyes.

"Sure, I can do that." Walt stared hard at a pile of trash not far from the door of the warehouse.

"Not a word, Walt."

"Not a word." He nodded, then clenched his hands together behind his back. "But if you wouldn't mind just getting the door for me, that would be very helpful."

"Yes, I'll get it." Jo pulled open the door, and held it open for him.

From the outside the warehouse appeared rundown and abandoned, but the inside was completely different. It was packed from wall to wall with luxury items, from plush couches, to gold tinted tables, to elaborate light displays. The wide-open floor was dotted with casino games of different styles.

"What is this place?" Walt gasped as he looked around.

"Not a word, Walt." Jo raised a finger in the air.

He coughed.

Jo walked towards the main stage where a band had begun to set up for live music. With each step her heart pounded faster. This was a lifestyle she didn't lead anymore, and she didn't like being sucked back into it. Not only was it dangerous for her mental state, it was dangerous in general. If any of her connections suspected that she had become an asset to the police, they might decide to get rid of the risk. She shot a brief look in Walt's direction and was relieved to see that he wore a stoic expression. When she turned her attention back to the stage she spotted the man she was looking for.

"Calvert!" She waved her hand through the air.

Calvert barely reached five feet tall. He was dressed impeccably in a high-end suit with shoes that likely cost more than everything Jo owned.

"Jo?" He squinted through the flickering lights. "Is that you?"

"Yes, it's me." She paused at the edge of the stage. As he walked towards her, she smiled. Calvert liked to have the higher ground, that was something she knew about him. The stage allowed him to tower over her.

"What are you doing here, Jo?" His eyes narrowed. "You don't belong here."

"No, you're right, I don't." Jo slipped her hand into her pocket, pulled out a few twenties, and set them down on the stage by his perfectly polished shoe. He didn't need the money, but if she had any chance of getting the information she knew she needed to give him some. It was a gesture of respect. "I just need a little information."

"Who's this?" He tipped his head towards Walt.

"I'm her bodyguard." Walt spoke up, though his voice wavered slightly.

"You?" Calvert laughed as his gaze swept over Walt's slight frame. "I doubt that."

Jo closed her eyes for just a second and summoned patience again. She looked straight at Calvert.

"He's not important. All I need to know is if anyone has sold you this vase." She held out her phone.

"Ah, isn't it beautiful." Calvert pursed his lips and offered a low whistle as he studied the picture. "Why are you after it?"

"You know how it is, Calvert. It's the one that got away." Jo smiled up at him. "I don't want to steal it. I just want to buy it."

"With what?" He laughed and shook his head. "You can't afford this, not with those shoes and those jeans."

"Can you just tell me who might have it?" Jo frowned, well aware that her cover story was falling apart.

"I didn't buy it, I can tell you that." He raised an eyebrow. "That vase is hotter than a stroll across the sun. I'm not that stupid. Besides I couldn't even prove it wasn't a replica, without getting some unwanted attention."

"But someone did try to sell it to you?" Jo took her phone back and met his eyes. "I just want the vase, Calvert, that's all."

"I bet." He crouched down so that he was at eye level with her, and spoke in a low but hard tone. "If you think I'm going to start working with the cops now, you've lost your mind."

"I'm not a cop." Jo's heartbeat quickened. "You know that."

"Yeah, I do. And I also know that he's not your bodyguard." He shot a brief glare in Walt's direction. "So, before you come into my place of business, you might want to think about what you're getting yourself into." He signaled two men that flanked doors near the back of the warehouse. The men were easily the size of two people each. They began to walk towards Jo and Walt.

"Wait, Calvert." Jo caught his hand, and attempted to meet his eyes. "Don't you remember what I did for you?"

"Water under the bridge, Jo." Calvert sighed, but he didn't pull his hand away.

"More like blood." Jo tightened her grasp on his hand, just enough to make it clear that she wasn't afraid.

"You haven't changed a bit, Jo." He laughed and waved off the two men. "Fine. You want to know who stole the vase?"

"Yes. I do." Jo leaned a little closer to him, without releasing his hand. "I need to know."

"Honestly, at first I thought it would be you. But when he showed up, I wasn't surprised." Calvert leaned closer to her as well, so close that she could smell the scent of cigarettes on his breath. "I thought maybe you two were working together on this. You know he would do anything to get that vase."

"Denver?" Jo gasped as she abruptly drew her hand back.

"You said it, not me." Calvert winked at her, then straightened up.

"Are you sure it was him? Did you see him yourself?" Jo searched his eyes for any hint of deceit.

"I've got no reason to lie about it. But like I said, I didn't buy it from him. That vase is too hot, and it's bad luck. If you want my advice, you should stay away from it too, Jo. I hear you've got yourself a squeaky clean, new life. You should stick with that." Calvert glanced over at Walt.

"Thanks for the information." Jo licked her lips, then steadied herself on the edge of the stage. "Do you happen to know where he's staying?"

"Of course, I don't." Calvert rolled his eyes. "You know better than that. But if I see him again, I can tell him that you're looking for him. Would you like that?"

"Yes, thank you." Jo drew back from the stage, then turned to face Walt. "Let's go."

"Wait, I might be able to get a little more information out of him." He started to turn back.

"No." Jo caught his hand and tugged him away from the stage. "The conversation is over."

CHAPTER 13

"What was that all about?" Walt spoke up the moment Jo stepped on the gas.

"I needed to find out who might have tried to steal the vase." She shrugged. "Now I know."

"That's not what I meant. What does that man owe you? How do you know Denver?" Walt leaned a little closer to her. "I'd like to hear the whole story."

"One day." Jo nodded, though she had no intention of sharing. However, as she neared Sage Gardens, she realized that she wouldn't have much choice in the matter. In order to share the information she'd discovered with the rest of her friends, she was going to have to tell them more than she would like to. Her heart skipped a beat at the thought of Denver being nearby. He likely wasn't. He'd probably swept in, killed Shayla, and left the country. As much as she wanted him to be caught, she still felt some relief at the idea that he was long gone.

"Jo."

Walt's soft voice pulled her out of her wild thoughts.

"We're almost there." She rubbed the back of her hand across her forehead.

"I know that." Walt tipped his head to the side as he gazed at her. "Are you okay?"

"I will be." Jo shot a brief glance in his direction. "I'll be fine."

"Who is he? Denver?" Walt shifted closer to her on the seat.

"Not now." Jo turned into Sage Gardens.

"You can always talk to me, Jo." Walt cleared his throat. "You know that right?"

"I know, Walt, thanks." Jo tightened her lips as she drove in the direction of Samantha's villa. She could always talk to Walt, but would he want to hear what she had to say?

Jo parked on the side of the road in front of Samantha's villa, as the driveway was already full.

She took a deep breath then flipped through her phone. A familiar face stared up at her. It was a face she would never forget. She stepped out of the car, with Walt right behind her. When she pushed open the front door, she spotted Eddy straight away. She had no idea how he would react, but she couldn't let that stop her from telling the truth. Justice for Shayla was more important than keeping her own secrets. She needed to let them know who to look out for in order to protect their safety.

"Denver." Jo tossed the phone down in the middle of the table, with the photograph still displayed. "We have our killer."

"Denver?" Eddy looked up at her, his eyes wide. "Is that supposed to mean something to me?"

"Not to you, no." Jo shook her head. "But if you mentioned it to the FBI, it would mean a whole lot."

"Wait a minute, what are you talking about?" Samantha peered at the picture as well. "Is this someone you know?"

"Knew." Jo stared down at the photograph. "Not well. More by reputation, than anything. I usually work alone, but there was one big job. I could never do it alone. So, we did just one job together." She glanced up at Eddy, as she knew talk of her past could make him uncomfortable. "He was the first person I thought of when that vase went missing."

"Why is that?" Eddy met her eyes.

"Because that one job he worked with me." Jo cleared her throat, glanced between the curious faces of her friends, then took a deep breath. "It was an attempt to steal the same vase."

"You're just telling us this now?" Eddy jumped up from his chair so fast that its legs scraped across the kitchen floor. "Jo! We needed to know that right away."

"No, you didn't." Jo crossed her arms, then pursed her lips. Denver stared up at her from the photograph. "We didn't get it, all right? I wasn't sure it was him, I wanted to get confirmation before I made an accusation."

"We should tell Detective Cooper right away. This is great news." Walt smiled and patted the curve of Jo's shoulder. "Now we have a main suspect, the pressure will be off Jo."

"Think that through, Walt." Eddy glared at him.

"Eddy, calm down." Samantha frowned, then looked back at Jo. "You really should have told us, Jo, if you even suspected. Does anyone know that you and Denver tried to steal it before?"

"We weren't caught if that's what you're asking."

Jo frowned. "Only a few people who knew us at the time know about it. I don't know who they might have told, though."

"Detective Cooper knows. That's for sure." Eddy smacked his hand on the table and groaned. "No wonder he's been digging into you so hard. He knows you were involved in one of the last attempts to steal the vase. He probably isn't even considering Denver, because you live right here, right down the street from where the vase was stolen, and a woman was murdered."

"I know." Jo slid her hands into her pockets as she braced herself for Eddy's fury. "I know I made a mistake, Eddy. I guess, I hoped it wasn't him."

"And you kept it from us." Eddy shook his head, then stared at her. "If you had told us from the beginning we could have protected you better. So why didn't you?"

"Enough." Walt slid his arm around Jo's shoulders. "That's enough, Eddy. Jo doesn't have to tell us everything. We all have our secrets."

"Yes, but most of them aren't grand larceny!" Eddy rolled his eyes and turned away from both of them.

"Okay, we all just need to take a breath here." Samantha held up her hands. "Walt is right. This is good news. We do have a main suspect. It may not be Detective Cooper's main suspect, but it's a solid lead. But Eddy is right too, telling Detective Cooper about this connection right now might not be the best idea, especially after the way I yelled at him. So, let's just try to figure out how we can get some proof that Denver is the murderer. Is he a violent man, Jo?"

Jo was grateful for Walt's arm around her shoulders. She wasn't the least bit afraid of Eddy, but the man who stared up at her from the table terrified her.

"Yes." She bit into her bottom lip.

"What aren't you telling us, now?" Eddy turned back to face her. "There's more, I can hear it in your voice, Jo. I thought I gave you enough reason to trust me."

"Eddy." Walt stared hard into his eyes.

"It's okay." Jo took a breath. "I'm the reason we weren't able to steal the vase. I wanted it, so bad. It was going to be my way out. The money I made from that would be enough for me to start a new life. But no one would take the risk with me. Then Denver showed up. He was the only one willing to do it. We thought the house would be empty." She looked up at Eddy. "But when we got there it wasn't. We came across a couple sleeping in their bed. Denver wanted to kill them, but I set off their alarm before he could. We ran, and that was it." She shrugged as Walt's arm tightened around her. "We didn't get the vase."

"But you saved their lives." Samantha gazed at her with warmth in her eyes. "If you hadn't been there —"

"If I hadn't gone after the vase in the first place, they never would have been in danger." Jo shivered. "I was the one who knew where the vase was. I was the one that led him to it. I was the one who thought the house would be empty."

"And you are the one who set off the alarm." Eddy sat back down in his chair. "You did the right thing, even though you knew you were putting yourself at risk. I'd guess that Denver wasn't too pleased with your stunt."

"That doesn't matter." Jo took a deep breath. "All that matters is that yes, I think that Denver went after the vase, and yes, I think that he is capable of murder."

Samantha shifted in her chair as the tension built in the air around the table. She could sense that Eddy was still riled up, and Jo had more than one emotion driving the scowl on her face. Walt's anger was palpable as he stared at the picture on the phone.

"A man like that shouldn't be allowed to roam free."

"No, he shouldn't." Jo bit into her bottom lip. "I need to go." She snatched up her phone.

"Jo, don't run off and do something on your own." Eddy snapped his head in her direction. "This man is dangerous, and he has a grudge against you, the last thing you should do is get in contact with him."

"He has a grudge against me, that's exactly the point. That might be the only reason that he's still around, if he is. If I try to set up a meeting with him, he might actually come out of hiding for it. I might be the only person that could catch him at this point." Jo placed her hands on her hips. "If that's not what you want, then too bad, because that's my plan."

"Jo, slow down." Samantha frowned as she reached for her friend's hand. "It's not a bad plan, but it would be better if we do it together."

"It's not a bad plan?" Walt's eyes widened. "Are you kidding me? It's the worst plan. The man's a murderer!"

"That may be, but Jo is right, she is someone

who could draw him out. He's a man that knows how to disappear. If he hasn't vanished already, it's likely because he realized Jo was in the area. If that's the case, then maybe we can get him to talk long enough to get a confession out of him." Samantha glanced from Jo, to Walt, then over at Eddy. "What do you think, Eddy?"

"I think you're right." He nodded slowly.

"Eddy!" Walt gasped, then stabbed his finger through the air in Eddy's direction. "You know better than anyone what a risk this would be."

"It doesn't have to be." Eddy ran his hand along his face and sighed. "We can get Detective Cooper on board with a meet-up. If so, we'll have all the backup we need."

"It's still a risk." Walt crossed his arms.

"It's a risk I'm willing to take. Honestly, it's more of a risk to me if he's out running around. Don't you think he might have a particular reason for sticking around here?" Jo stared straight into Walt's eyes. "I appreciate your desire to protect me, but it's important that you don't forget I am capable of taking care of myself, and making decisions for myself, like this one. It's my choice, and I am willing to take the risk. I'd rather not work with Detective Cooper, but if you all think that would be for the best, I am willing to consider it."

"I think it would be." Samantha released her hand and smiled as she glanced over at Eddy. "It would be a great way to wipe your name off the suspect list, Jo, and a good way for Eddy to bond with him. Not to mention the fact that if he messes anything up, he already knows that he has me to answer to."

"She makes a good point." Eddy grinned, then looked across the table at Walt. "So, what do you say, pal?"

"Does my opinion even count?" Walt directed his question to the group, but his eyes settled on Jo.

"Of course it does." Jo frowned. "I'd like to know that I'll have your support."

"You'll always have my support." Walt sighed and held his hands out in a gesture of surrender.

"Great, it's decided then. Eddy, can you set up a meeting with Detective Cooper?" Samantha pulled out her phone. "Let's make sure that we can get this rolling as soon as possible."

"Yes, I'll see what I can do." Eddy pulled out his own phone.

"I'm going to see if I can get hold of Troy, there are a few things I want to ask him about." Samantha began to call as she waved to Jo who disappeared through the front door.

Walt stared at both of them, shook his head, then turned and walked out of the villa.

"He's not happy." Eddy cringed, then turned his attention back to his phone.

"He will be, once Jo is out of danger." Samantha stared after Walt until Troy answered the phone.

"Hi Troy. It's Samantha Smith from Sage Gardens." She did her best to infuse a smile into her voice.

"Samantha, right. How are you?" He paused.

"I'd like to meet up with you. I wanted to get some ideas for the memorial. Since I didn't know your mother, I thought maybe you could give me some suggestions. Can we get coffee or something?"

"Uh, I guess. Yes, that would be fine. When?"

"Now?" Samantha glanced at the time on the clock on the wall. "Or as soon as you can? We could meet at the diner?"

"Sure. I can be there in a few minutes." His voice wavered some, but not enough to indicate stress.

"Thanks Troy. See you soon." Samantha hung up the phone just as Eddy hung up his. "I'm meeting

Troy for coffee. Did you get through to Detective Cooper?"

"No, I think I'm just going to go down there." Eddy shrugged. "It's better than leaving a message."

"Okay, great." Samantha grabbed her purse. "We'll meet back here after?"

"Sounds good." Eddy walked out of the villa ahead of her.

Samantha waved to him as he pulled out of the driveway. She settled in her own car and narrowed her eyes. Yes, Denver was a great suspect. But that didn't mean he was the killer. What about the frustrated son who was willing to steal from his mother? What about the missing steel car that would be pretty much worthless to anyone but him? What about the picture frame?"

Samantha was at the diner within minutes. The waitress from that morning was still there and gave her a quick smile as she headed for a busy table.

Samantha spotted Troy not far from the window. She sat down at his table and smiled.

"Thanks so much for meeting me, and so quickly." She slipped her phone out of her purse.

"It's no problem. I'm kind of stuck here, at least until things are resolved with my mother." Troy leaned his chin on his hand and stared at her. "So, what did you need?"

"I was hoping to get some more people together that knew Shayla. Do you know this man?" Samantha passed her phone across the table to Troy. She'd created a still photograph from the television show footage.

"In the picture?" He glanced from it, up to Samantha, and then back down again. "Yes, of course I know him. That's Uncle Brad."

"Uncle Brad?" She raised an eyebrow. "Your mother's brother?"

"No. Well, not really. I always called him uncle. But he was just a good friend of hers. They spent a lot of time together when I was younger. For a while, anyway." Troy pushed the phone back across the table. "Why do you want to know about him?"

"Why only for a while? Did they part ways at some point?" Samantha turned the screen on her phone off.

"Yeah, I guess. I mean, he was over every day, then suddenly he didn't come back." Troy shrugged.

"Did your mother ever mention her feelings for him?" She leaned a little closer. "Maybe more than friendship?"

"No. It wasn't like that with them. Not at all. I

just figured he got tired of how weird she was. It was around that time that she started really packing the house up with stuff. A lot of her friends backed away. It was too much for most people to handle." Troy took a long swallow of his soda.

"It must have been so hard on you." Samantha frowned. "I bet you couldn't have friends over, girl-friends?"

"No way. I didn't even tell people where I lived. But people still found out, eventually. It got a little better after high school, everyone was so distracted with their lives, but then there was the fire." Troy winced. "And everyone had something to say about that."

"The fire?" Samantha looked up at him. "What fire?"

"One night a fire broke out in the house where I grew up. It was not long after Dad moved out. Honestly, there just wasn't room for him anymore. I already lived in my place. I don't know, I guess it was about ten years ago, now that I think of it. The fire broke out, and if it weren't for the sprinklers I had installed just in case, she would have burned right along with that house. That's when I realized just how dangerous it was for her to be living in that tinder box. I had hoped that moving to a new place would give her a fresh start, and she might be able to let go of the hoarding. But it didn't work out that way." Troy balled his hands into fists on the table. "For a few months, it wasn't too bad. Then she began to collect again. I tried to talk to her about it, but she would tell me that she lost almost everything, and I had no right to begrudge her a few treasures. Treasures." Troy rolled his eyes. "I'm sorry, Samantha, I know that you think I should be heartbroken, that I should be grateful for the memorial, but I honestly don't even want to be there." He stood up before the waitress could even walk over to take Samantha's order. "I need to go."

"I understand, Troy. If you change your mind, please know you're welcome to join us."

He nodded, but hurried out the door.

Instead of ordering anything, Samantha stood up and left as well.

CHAPTER 14

The sight of the man entering the police station had stopped Eddy cold in his tracks. He recognized him as Jacob, Shayla's estranged husband. His presence didn't appear voluntary, as an officer greeted him at the door and escorted him into the police station. Eddy put two and two together and assumed that Detective Cooper intended to interrogate Jacob. He decided not to interrupt. Instead he remained in the car and waited for Jacob to exit. If Detective Cooper had enough on him to arrest him, then he wouldn't come back out, but if he didn't, then he knew that Jacob would come right back through those doors.

About thirty minutes slid by. In the time that passed, Eddy read through the information that

Samantha sent him from her conversation with Troy.

"Uncle Brad, huh?" He raised an eyebrow as he recalled the man from their brief encounter inside the police station. He'd been questioned on the same day as the murder, which meant two things. Brad was top on Detective Cooper's radar soon after the murder, and he had been local enough to get to the station in a short amount of time. That coupled with his involvement with a previous murder investigation made him a fairly good suspect. However, Jacob's ability to profit from his wife's death made him a better suspect.

Eddy watched as the front door of the police station swung open. It seemed to be the right amount of time for an interrogation to be complete. An unsuccessful interrogation. As Eddy expected, Jacob descended the front steps. Eddy stepped out of the car just as Jacob began approaching his own car.

"Excuse me." Eddy gave him a quick wave.

"Yes?" Jacob paused beside his car and looked at Eddy. "What is it?"

"You wouldn't happen to have some jumper cables, would you?" He jerked his thumb over his shoulder. "I can't get the old girl started."

"Oh." Jacob glanced at his car, then back at Eddy. "I don't, but I'm sure they have some inside."

"Probably." Eddy winced, then tipped his head back and forth. "But I'd rather not ask. They hauled me in there just before to question me about some murder. I really have no idea why they decided to come after me, I'm not a murderer." He held up his hands. "I swear, I would never kill anybody."

"Listen, I really can't help you." Jacob slid one hand into his pocket. "I need to be somewhere."

"I get it, I must sound crazy." Eddy chuckled. "Who would want to help a murder suspect?"

"It's not that." Jacob shrugged. "I was in there facing the same questions. That detective doesn't have a clue." He rolled his eyes. "He just wants to waste his time flapping his gums."

"He's pathetic." Eddy nodded. He heard the subtle clink of keys knocking together in Jacob's pocket. "And now I'm stuck here. So, I guess that will look suspicious, too. Funny thing is, I've never even met the woman who died. I guess, she wasn't much of a talker."

"Oh, she could talk." Jacob rolled his eyes. "I was married to her. Trust me, she could talk."

"Oh no, I'm so sorry." Eddy extended his hand.

"I had no idea. Here I am talking like a fool about your wife. I'm very sorry for your loss."

"Thanks." Jacob gave his hand a firm shake. "But we were split up for a while. She and I didn't get along well. We stayed together for the kid, then of course that didn't work. So, we separated."

"Not divorced?" Eddy tilted his head to the side. "Didn't want to bite the bullet? Maybe there was still some love there?"

"No, it wasn't love. It was money. It's costly to get a divorce." Jacob kicked one shoe against the ground and shrugged. "She didn't care. It wasn't as if she had any chance of finding someone else."

"That's not what that detective said." Eddy laughed, then shook his head. "He kept asking me if I was seeing Shayla. Then he kept asking me if I'd seen this other guy around her. What was his name." He narrowed his eyes. "Brad, that was it. He kept asking me over and over again, did you ever see her with Brad? I kept telling him, I've never seen her at all."

"Brad?" Jacob straightened up and stared right at Eddy. "Are you sure that's the name the detective was asking about?"

"Yes, I'm sure. He kept repeating it. I just figured Brad must have been her friend or boyfriend or something." Eddy pulled his fedora off and ran his hand back through his hair. "Not sure why he kept asking me, though. I've never met a Brad."

"I have." Jacob clenched his jaw so tight that Eddy could see a ripple of the muscle through the skin on his cheek. "Brad Walton. He's a terrible person. I told Shayla she should stay away from him. If he was back in her life, then he's probably the one who killed her."

"You think so?" Eddy grinned. "So it wasn't you, right?"

"Right." Jacob jerked open his car door. "I can prove it to the cops, but I don't have to prove it to you." He slammed the door shut, then sped out of the parking lot. Eddy stared after him and wondered how he could prove that he was not the one who killed his wife. He hoped it was more than just his current girlfriend claiming that he was in bed with her all night. He texted Samantha Brad's full name, then looked up at the police station and decided that it was time to have that conversation with Detective Cooper.

As soon as Eddy stepped inside, he spotted the man near the front desk.

"Detective Cooper!" He walked towards him.

"Eddy." He turned around to face him. "What are you up to, now?"

"Not up to anything, sir, just would like a word with you if that's possible. I know how busy you are." Eddy pulled his hat off and held it between his hands.

"I am busy." Detective Cooper locked his eyes to Eddy's. "But I suppose I can spare a few minutes. Quickly." He gestured towards an empty desk.

"Great, thanks. I appreciate it." Eddy sat down in a chair in front of the desk. Detective Cooper joined him moments later.

"What is it?" He glanced at his watch, then back up at Eddy.

"Was that Shayla's ex that just left the police station?" Eddy folded his hands on the table and relaxed his shoulders. He assumed it wouldn't take long for Detective Cooper to get the message that he wasn't going to be rushed out the door.

"Yes, it was. A waste of time." Detective Cooper grimaced. "Time is something I don't have right now."

"Why was it a waste of time? I thought he was a prime suspect?" Eddy studied the man's harried expression. It seemed to him that this investigation was taking a toll on the detective.

"He was, but he has a solid alibi." He narrowed his eyes. "Why are you asking about him?"

"What alibi? I know his car went through the front gates of Sage Gardens after midnight, on the day that Shayla's body was found." Eddy stared right back at him.

"Oh, do you?" Detective Cooper leaned across the desk. "And just how do you know that?"

Eddy's heart pounded as he realized the mistake he'd made.

"That doesn't matter. How did you clear him?" He frowned.

"Yes, he was in Sage Gardens that night, and he was escorted out by the security guard. After which, he was at a nearby bar until closing, at which point the bartender put him into a taxi, which drove him to a local motel, where he checked in at the exact time of death that the medical examiner has recorded for Shayla. Throughout that span of time, he was never really out of sight, he only used the bathroom once. So, you tell me, how could he have killed his wife?" Detective Cooper shook his head. "He was a good suspect, but he's not the one who killed her. He returned to the complex in the morning on foot. He was apparently trying to get Shayla to give him money and he didn't want the security guard to escort him off the property again. It all adds up, he couldn't have killed her. Which brings me to a more important question. Where's Jo?" He locked his eyes to Eddy's.

"Actually, that's what I'm here to talk to you about." Eddy sat back in his chair and wondered if it was still a good idea to involve the detective. However, it seemed far too late now to change his mind.

It didn't take Samantha long to find an address for Uncle Brad. Once she knew his name, he was fairly easy to find. Since he was only a little over thirty minutes away, she decided to make the drive, and hope that he was home. Even if he wasn't she would at least have a chance to look at his house. She'd learned that houses could tell stories, and even reveal secrets. That's all she intended to do, take a look at the house, and find out what she could from it.

However, when she pulled up beside the house she noticed a car in the driveway. Could it be Brad's car? From her research it didn't appear that he was married. Perhaps, that had something to do with his past relationship with Shayla.

"Don't get out of the car, Samantha." She took a deep breath. "You're just here to take a look."

Samantha stared at the house for a few more moments, then popped open the car door. She crept towards the house, her steps punctuated by quick glances over her shoulder to see if anyone might spot her. Her intention was just to get a look through one of the windows. She just wanted an idea of how Brad lived. But instead, the front door swung open, and she was caught halfway up Brad's driveway.

"Hello?" Brad smiled as he stood just outside the door.

Samantha's heart raced. She hadn't prepared any lie about why she was there, as she had no intention of speaking to Brad. But there he was, with a warm smile on his lips, and curiosity in his eyes.

"Hi." She adjusted the strap of her purse on her shoulder. "I'm sorry to just drop in on you like this."

"It's quite all right. Is there something I can help you with?" Brad narrowed his eyes as he scrutinized her features. "Do I know you from somewhere?"

"No, I don't believe so. We have a mutual friend,

well sort of." Samantha laughed nervously, then looked into his eyes. She wanted to see his reaction as she said her next words. "Shayla Thompson."

He shifted from one foot to the other. His arms folded across his chest. But his eyes never left hers.

"Shayla? You were a friend of hers?" His brows knitted together.

"Actually, no. I didn't know her. But we lived in the same retirement community." Her stomach twisted. Why had she just told a potential killer where she lived? Had she really lost her edge that much?

"Oh, I see." Brad nodded, then unfolded his arms. He slid his hands into his pockets and continued to stare at her. "So, why are you here?"

"Oh yes, so sorry. Well, our community is having a memorial for Shayla tonight, and honestly I've had a hard time finding anyone that knew her well. Her son, Troy, isn't interested in participating." She watched his eyes again as she spoke Troy's name, but they didn't change. "And her estranged husband, Jacob, I'm just not sure that he will paint the best image of Shayla. So, when Troy mentioned his Uncle Brad, I just thought—"

"Troy mentioned me?" His eyebrows raised. "He spoke to you about me?"

"Yes, he said that you and his mother were very good friends, and so I thought you might like to be part of the memorial." Samantha tightened her grip on the strap of her purse. "It didn't seem like something that should be discussed over the phone."

"I'm surprised that Troy remembers me." Brad ran his hands back through his hair. "Shayla and I haven't been friends for some time. We fell out of touch and I haven't seen her for many years. Of course, I was still devastated to hear about her death."

"I'm very sorry for your loss." Samantha met his eyes. "I wish I'd had the chance to know her."

"She was a very interesting person. She was always so vibrant, so daring." Brad smiled more to himself, than towards her. "There was a time I thought I would never be able to keep up with her."

"It sounds like you knew her very well." Samantha did her best to hide her surprise from her expression. From what she knew of Shayla, she didn't think she could ever be described as daring and hard to keep up with. She didn't even leave her house. "It's hard when friendships fall to the wayside. I suppose family life made it hard to maintain her friendship with you."

"Ah, yes. Something like that." Brad nodded.

"Thanks for the invitation to the memorial, but I don't think I'll be able to make it. There are some things that need my attention this evening."

"I understand. I appreciate you just taking the time to talk with me. It was nice to get a glimpse of Shayla as you knew her. I mean, it's hard to see past her collections." Samantha tipped her head to the side. "She accumulated so much."

"Yes, she did." Brad cleared his throat. "I don't know how she lived like that. Her villa is so full of stuff. I could barely walk through it." He gestured to his car. "Sorry to leave abruptly, but I do have an appointment to get to."

"Oh yes of course, it's fine." Samantha stepped aside as he started down his driveway. For a moment she was tempted to linger, and perhaps take a peek in his windows after all. But she doubted that it would reveal much. Brad was a very put-together man. His clothes were nice, wrinkle-free, and complemented his frame. His yard was neat, with just enough color to be cheerful, without requiring a lot of maintenance. Even his car was just the right fit for him, and new, as well as spotless. She noticed the sun gleam off the blue paint as he pulled out of the driveway. She turned to watch him drive away, then jumped at the sound of a shrill ring in her purse. She dug through it and pulled out her phone.

"Hi Eddy. How did things go with Detective Cooper?"

"Not great." Eddy sighed. "Our favorite suspect is no longer a suspect at all." He filled her in on Jacob's alibi.

"It's a little wobbly." Samantha frowned. "It's possible that someone is lying. But I have to admit, it's more solid than I would like."

"I think we need to at least consider that someone else might be the killer. My next best guess is Troy. He was there that evening, and he could have easily been the one to do it." Eddy clucked his tongue. "I'd hate to think of a son killing his mother."

"Me too. But it sounds like we need to consider it. Of course, we have another suspect that has a tendency to be violent. Denver." Samantha scrunched up her nose at the sound of his name. Even speaking it made her feel uneasy. She didn't know him, herself, but she could tell from the way Jo spoke about him, he was a terrible person.

"That's true. Detective Cooper agreed to work with me and Jo to set up a sting for Denver. But he did so reluctantly." Eddy's tone grew tense. "It took quite a bit of convincing."

"Do you think that we can trust him? Will he keep Jo safe?" Samantha frowned as she walked towards her car.

"I wouldn't even be considering it if I didn't trust him to keep her safe. The question is, will she really be willing to participate?"

CHAPTER 15

Only one bar in town sold Denver's favorite alcohol. Jo knew exactly what he liked to drink. Back when she was a novice thief, when she had admired him, she had learned everything she could about him. If he was still in town, and she suspected that he was, she knew that he would be at the place where he could get his favorite drink. A rare whisky. When Jo pushed open the door and peered into the dimly lit space, she spotted him at the far end of the bar. More silver hair than brown, and his shoulders had rounded, but it was definitely him. In that moment, she hesitated. She could turn and walk away. She could pretend that she never saw him, never found him. But she knew it was already too late for that. There was no way she could walk away from him, when she believed he might be responsible for Shayla's death.

As Jo walked up to the bar, Denver turned his head towards her, and smiled, as if he'd known she was coming the whole time.

"Jo." He gestured to the stool next to him.

"Denver." Jo took a short breath as she sat down beside him.

The bartender placed a shot glass down in front of Denver, then darted off to other customers.

"I heard you were looking for me." He downed the liquid in the shot glass, then set the glass down hard on the bar. "Another." He flicked his wrist towards the bartender, who hurried to fulfill his request.

"I found you." Jo twisted on the bar stool next to his. Just being near him was enough to stir up all kinds of anxiety within her. Once she had admired him. He'd pulled off more impossible jobs than anyone she knew. But that had all changed when they had worked together. She knew that he didn't have any affection for her, either. In fact, after she'd set off the alarm that day when they worked together, he'd sworn that he would make her pay for it. He hadn't yet. But she also hadn't given him the opportunity. She'd been avoiding him ever since.

"But why?" Denver tilted his head to the side as he looked at her. "Remarkable." His gaze raked along her features, and her figure, then he shook his head slowly.

"What do you mean remarkable?" She glanced at him, then turned her attention to the bottles of alcohol that lined the wall behind the bar. She didn't want to drink. She also didn't want to be perched next to the man that had likely killed Shayla.

"You haven't aged a day." Denver shifted on the bar stool, then slid his hand along the top of the bar until it collided with hers. "I had such a crush on you back then."

"A crush?" Jo laughed as she cringed inside. "What, are we in grade school?"

"Okay fine." He took a deep breath. "I adored everything about you."

"That's not true." Jo scrunched up her nose. "You barely spoke to me."

"Because I was so nervous." Denver chuckled. "I wanted to impress you so badly."

"Impress me?" Jo rested her chin on her hand. "Are you sure that you don't have me confused with someone else?" Her heart skipped a beat as he reached for a strand of her dark hair that had fallen into her line of vision.

"Oh no, I could never forget you, Jo." Denver swept the hair back behind her ear, then gave her cheek a light pat. "You're the only person who ever betrayed me, and lived. So far." He cast a wink in her direction.

"I'm not afraid of you, Denver." Jo infused her voice with confidence, confidence that didn't actually exist.

"Yes, you are." Denver stared down at his glass. "You're terrified. And you should be." He glanced up at her. "But I'm not going to hurt you, Jo. Not now." He shrugged. "I need you."

"You need me? For what?" Jo looked over at him, and braced herself for what his response might be. Did he want her to help him with a job?

"I need you to find out who framed me." He ran his fingertip along the rim of the glass.

Jo stared at him in silence as she tried to work out his intentions.

"Framed you for what?" She took a sharp breath.

"Don't pretend that you don't know." Denver slid the glass along the bar, then glanced up at her. "I know why you're here. You know why I'm here. Let's not waste time pretending."

"You expect me to believe that you were framed

for Shayla's murder?" Jo smirked, then shook her head. "I know you better than that, Denver. No one cons you."

"You did." Denver sat back some on the bar stool and turned to fully face her. "I'm not playing games here, Jo. I'm stuck in this nothing town, and you happen to be here, too? Did you think you could frame me, then get the vase from me?"

"You think I framed you?" Her muscles tensed as she began to see things through his eyes. It was a stretch, but if she were him, she might suspect the same thing.

"You, or somebody else." He closed his eyes for a moment, just long enough for her to notice the deep lines in his face and the heaviness around his eyes. Yes, he had aged. She couldn't see it unless she looked closely, but the evidence was there. Was that why he had come after the vase? One final job.

"Where is Jo?" Walt looked up from his computer at the sound of Eddy's voice as he pushed open the door to Walt's villa. He hadn't even knocked.

"Eddy?" He stood up from his desk. "What's wrong?"

"I've been trying to reach Jo. She's not answering her phone. She's supposed to meet up with me to set up a trap for Denver. Detective Cooper is expecting us." Eddy crossed his arms as his eyes settled on Walt. "You need to tell me where she is."

"I have no idea." Walt frowned, as his eyes widened. "Are you saying you can't get in contact with her?"

"I've been to her place, she's not there, and neither is her car." Eddy turned back towards the door. "I'm going to check at Samantha's, she's not home yet, but maybe Jo is waiting for her there."

"She would answer her phone if she was there." Walt began to pace. "If she's not answering then it can only mean one of two things. She turned her phone off because she's up to something she shouldn't be, or she's not able to answer it because someone else is stopping her."

"You think she could be in danger?" Eddy turned around to face him.

"I think she wanted to find Denver." Walt shuddered. "What if she found him?"

"She was supposed to wait for me, so that the police could keep her safe." Eddy narrowed his eyes.

"When have you ever known Jo to follow directions?" Walt slammed his fist into his palm. "I never should have let her go off alone." He sighed and shook his head.

"Let's not get ahead of ourselves. We don't know that she's gone after Denver, or that she found him, or that he's done anything to her. Let me call Samantha." Eddy fished his phone out of his pocket. "Remember, we don't even know if Denver is the killer."

"I know it wasn't Troy, and Jacob has already been cleared." Walt frowned as he called Jo's number.

"Wait, what? How do you know it wasn't Troy?" Eddy pressed his phone against his ear and listened to the ringing.

"I looked more thoroughly through his bank records that you got for me. He made a purchase at a gas station twenty miles away from Shayla's villa at the time of her death. So, I called the gas station to see if they remembered him, and the clerk did. He claimed that Troy was there for over an hour shouting on the phone with someone about a toy car. That would stick out in anyone's mind I think." Walt shook his head as Jo's voicemail picked up. "She's not answering. If it wasn't Jacob, and it wasn't Troy, then it has to be Denver. If Jo's not answering, and she didn't show up for your meeting, then something is wrong! What are we going to do?"

"I'll see if Detective Cooper can help. I know he's been on the lookout for Denver. If he has an idea of where Denver is, maybe we can track down Jo." Eddy paused as Samantha answered the phone. "Hang on, Sam, give me one second." He looked back at Walt. "I'll let you know what Detective Cooper says. For now, just keep calling Jo. Let me know if you reach her."

"All right, I will." Walt frowned.

"Sam? Yes, Jo's missing. I'm on the way to check if she's at your villa, and if not I'll go to the police station to see if Detective Cooper can help."

Eddy stepped through the door and pulled it closed behind him.

Walt started to call Jo's number again, but he hung up before it went through. There was no point to calling repeatedly and getting the same result. He sat back down at his computer and attempted to access Jo's bank account. He was a retired accountant and she had recently asked him to look at how she had her accounts set up. He didn't want to invade his friend's privacy, but this was an emergency. With the username suggested from previously being filled in on his computer, he used his knowledge of Jo to guess at her password, and relatively quickly managed to get through. It was one of her favorite flowers, petunias, and her birth day and month.

"A recent purchase at Hilltop Bar." He narrowed his eyes. He knew that Jo rarely drank, and when she did, it wasn't in the middle of the day at a bar. "What were you doing there, Jo?" He grabbed his keys. "I'm going to find out." As he started towards the door, he pictured the inside of a seedy bar. A shiver raced up his spine. He turned around and grabbed an extra pack of sanitizing wipes, hand sanitizer and some gloves. Satisfied, he left his villa. For a moment he thought about calling Eddy, and letting him know what he discovered. But he knew if he did Eddy would want to tell Detective Cooper. He wasn't quite sure what Jo was up to, and he didn't want to risk making things worse if the police showed up.

On his drive to the bar, he played out all of the possible outcomes in his mind. Usually, doing so soothed him. This time, it only worked him into more of an anxious state. There was only one good outcome, that Jo was just fine and everything had been a mistake. But that was the least likely outcome, and Walt made decisions based on statistics and evidence. Which left him only with scenarios that didn't end well. He stepped on the gas, and broke the speed limit, something he never did.

"Jo, whatever is going on, I'm coming to help!"

CHAPTER 16

*a*fter not finding Jo at Samantha's villa, Eddy headed for the police station. He had to face Detective Cooper and tell him that the plan they agreed on was off. After the revelation, Detective Cooper rolled his eyes.

"Not surprising to me. Once a criminal always a criminal. How do you know the two didn't run off together?"

"Jo would never do that." Eddy frowned. "Could you please let me know if you find any sign of Denver? I'm concerned about her."

"Sure, fine." The detective waved his hand. "Anything else? I have to get back to work."

"Can I get the old case file from the murder

investigation that Shayla was involved in?" Eddy perched on the edge of the chair, and watched as Detective Cooper pretended to ignore him.

"Our agreement was you help me, I keep you informed." He finally looked up from the file on his desk. "You didn't fulfill your end."

"Sure, I did." Eddy shrugged as he studied the man. "Jo spoke to you, didn't she?"

"Right, and we were supposed to work together to catch Denver, now she's vanished. And your friend Samantha shouted at me in public." Detective Cooper flipped the file shut, sighed, then fixed his gaze on Eddy. "Listen, I understand that you don't want to let go of this job. I can't even imagine a time when I would turn in my badge. I have no idea who I would be if I wasn't a cop. But you aren't anymore. You're retired. It's my job to get to the bottom of all of this. Your visits, your calls, they're just serving as a distraction right now, and I need them to stop."

"I get it. You don't want me meddling. I wouldn't want some retired old fool cutting into any of my cases if I were in your shoes. But that's not what I'm doing here. I just want to look into something. I don't want to distract you, and I certainly can't solve the case for you, that's your job." Eddy spread his hands out in front of him. "I'm just asking for a favor."

"Ah, I see. Trying to stroke my ego." Detective Cooper leaned across his desk. "Eddy, there's nothing to find in Shayla's past. I've been through all of it with a fine-tooth comb. There's nothing to find. So, you're wasting your time, and my time, by even having this conversation."

"It's not a waste." Eddy stood up from his chair. "I'm sorry to bother you, Detective Cooper. I have other ways to get what I need."

"Fine! Here." Detective Cooper pulled open a drawer on his desk, then slapped a file down on the desk in front of him. "This is the old case file. Feel free to pick it apart. Now, could you please call off Samantha? She said she was going to put in an official complaint about me, and I don't want the hassle of dealing with it."

"Don't worry. She's harmless." Eddy picked up the file.

"That I don't believe for a second." Detective Cooper shot him a brief look of annoyance. "Just get her to calm down, will you?"

"She will. As soon as you stop treating Jo like a

suspect." Eddy tucked the file under his arm. "She isn't one."

"She was there, she has a history, and she has a connection to the most valuable item that was stolen from the villa. Until I can prove otherwise she absolutely is a suspect. You might not like that, but I wouldn't be doing my job, if that wasn't the case, and you know it."

"That may be true." Eddy nodded slowly. "But it doesn't change the fact that she's innocent. You can solve this, Detective Cooper, but only if you're willing to follow your instincts. If you chase down every lead just for the sake of chasing it, you'll miss out on the truth. Jo may look suspicious, but I think your gut tells you she's not. Otherwise you wouldn't have met her for coffee, you wouldn't have tolerated Samantha yelling at you, you wouldn't have asked me to speak to her, instead of just showing up at her villa and handcuffing her."

"Point taken, Eddy." Detective Cooper looked into his eyes as he stood up from his desk. "But even if she is innocent, that doesn't solve the crime, does it? I have work to do." He gestured to the door.

"Right. Thanks for this." Eddy waved the file at him, then tucked it under his arm again.

As Eddy drove to Samantha's, he searched the streets for any sign of Jo. He'd told Walt not to worry, but the truth was, he was concerned. It wasn't like Jo not to communicate. She'd worked hard to gain the trust of her friends, and Eddy knew that she wanted to keep it. His nerves bristled at the thought of Detective Cooper still considering her a suspect. Had she gotten spooked and taken off? He gritted his teeth as he realized that might be the case.

When he knocked on Samantha's door, she was there to open it.

"Come in, Eddy, have you heard anything from Jo?"

"No." Eddy frowned and sat down at the kitchen table. "Sam, maybe she took off." He flipped open the file.

"She wouldn't do that." Samantha crossed her arms.

"Unless she thought she might be arrested for murder." Eddy glanced up at her with a grim expression. "We can't know for sure, can we?"

"I know for sure." Samantha opened up her computer. "And I'm going to find her. Friends don't just disappear. I found out who Gina Post is."

"You did?"

"It's Bunny's sister. She was visiting Bunny so

late because Gina's getting married and wanted to call it off, Bunny told her to come over so they could talk it through. Bunny is very excited that she is still getting married. I'm not sure if she is more concerned about her sister's happiness or the party. So, we can exclude her as a suspect."

"Good work, Sam." Eddy nodded. "Do you have a still photograph of the picture frame that was stolen?" Eddy looked up at her.

"I do." She pulled it up on her phone. "Why?"

"Shayla and Brad parted ways years ago, not long after the murder investigation. Between what Troy told us, and what Brad told us, I was able to figure that out. But until now, I couldn't understand why the picture frame might have been stolen. The vase is supposedly priceless, and the toy car was part of a valuable collection, and may have had sentimental value for Troy. But we've gotten nowhere on the picture frame. We still have no idea if it's even valuable."

"Well, maybe the thief just grabbed it as a little bonus." Samantha shrugged as she showed him the photograph.

"I knew it." Eddy's eyes narrowed. "See that Ferris wheel they're standing in front of? It was the Ferris wheel by the town center. It is closed down now." He pointed to the banner at the gates of the wheel in the background of the picture. "It says 'Grand Opening'."

"Okay?" Samantha narrowed her eyes. "And?"

"And, if I'm not mistaken that Ferris wheel opened in the same year of this murder investigation. Can you check on that?"

"Sure." Samantha did a quick search. "Yes, it opened in the same year in the same month." She looked up at Eddy.

"There it is." Eddy sat back in his chair and stared at the file. "I can't believe it, but there it is."

"What do you mean? There what is?" Samantha tilted her chair forward as she attempted to figure out what he saw in the photograph.

"According to Brad's statement, he was three states away when this murder took place." Eddy tapped the file in front of him. "He claimed that he'd gone away for business for a few months, and that he hadn't returned until after the murder of his business partner. But that was at the same time when the Ferris wheel had its grand opening, and this picture was taken."

"And the picture was taken in the same city as the murder." Samantha's eyes widened.

"Yes, it was. Shayla's statement indicates that

she had not seen Brad for weeks. But according to this picture, they were likely together on the same weekend that the murder took place." He shook his head slowly. "She lied to protect him."

"We're making a lot of assumptions here, Eddy." Samantha frowned. "There are other possibilities."

"There are. But why else would the photograph have been stolen from Shayla's home? It's proof that he lied to the police, proof that he was in the same city where his business partner was killed, proof that he had a reason to falsify an alibi." Eddy raised an eyebrow as he looked up at Samantha. "That sounds like a pretty good motive to me."

"I was just with him. He said he had an appointment to get to. He claimed he was heartbroken over Shayla's death. Oh!" Samantha clapped a hand over her mouth as she gasped. "He also said that her villa was so crowded he could barely walk through it. But he claimed they had been out of touch for years! He must have been there recently. He lied! And he might have seen the photograph on the television show." Samantha snapped her fingers. "He might have seen it, then decided he had to get it and destroy it. Maybe, he decided to kill the only other person that knew about his lies, too. Or maybe she wouldn't let him take it and he had to kill her to get it."

"Maybe. I need to call Detective Cooper about this." Eddy picked up his phone, then headed out onto the porch. His heart pounded as he realized that the case might actually be solved. But was it too late to catch the killer?

After hitting a dead end at the bar, in the form of a very uncooperative bartender, Walt sat in his car. His instincts told him that something was wrong. Jo was in trouble. She still didn't answer her phone. He gripped the steering wheel and squeezed it as his frustration mounted. Where was she? Had Denver taken her somewhere? Or worse? He was tempted to go back into the bar and threaten to knock out the bartender, but he wasn't Eddy. It would be an empty threat. The bartender would laugh it off, and he would have wasted more time.

Walt had no idea how to track down Denver. He closed his eyes, and instantly Shayla's crowded villa popped into his mind. In all of that clutter, perhaps Denver had left something behind. Maybe there would be some clue as to his whereabouts, or at the very least a way to track him. It was the only option he could think of, after all, Denver had been there. He'd stolen the vase, that much he knew for sure. Whether or not he murdered Shayla, he certainly had plenty of motive to harm Jo.

As Walt drove to Shayla's villa, he ignored a call from Eddy. He didn't want to hear from anyone but Jo. Eddy would likely just tell him not to worry. People always told him not to worry. As if it was something he could control, as if a compulsion that had affected him his entire life, could just be shut off, because someone told him not to worry. His brain had already calculated the statistical outcome of Jo's potential abduction, and tears threatened his eyes. She couldn't be dead. He wouldn't believe it, even if it was the most logical answer.

Walt's chest ached as he parked in front of Shayla's villa.

Entering it again seemed like a terrible idea. The germs, the dust, it would be even worse. But he knew it was what he had to do. He grabbed a face mask from the supply he kept in his car, and donned the gloves that he'd tucked into his pocket. If there was a clue that would lead him to Denver, he would find it.

As he approached the front door, he noticed that

the police tape had been pulled down. It was still there, but it had been moved to create enough room to enter the villa. Before he could think about it too much, he heard a thump from inside the villa. His heart skipped a beat. Was someone inside? When he pressed his hand against the front door, it swung open beneath the pressure. He stared at the narrow opening created, and held his breath. If someone was inside, they would notice he was there, wouldn't they? He glanced over his shoulder in the direction of the street. No police cars came charging down the road. He didn't notice anyone else around.

"Jo? Are you in there?" He poked his head through the small opening. "Jo? It's me, Walt!"

He heard another flutter of sound, as if something had fallen, and then a crash. His heart began to race. Yes, it would make sense for Denver to bring Jo back to Shayla's villa. Maybe he was trying to pin the murder on her. Maybe he thought if she was found in the villa with the vase she would be the one to go down for murder. Walt couldn't let that happen.

"Jo!" Walt charged into the house and ran down the partially cleared hallway in the direction of the crash. As he rounded a corner, he came face-to-face with a mountain of clutter. It was taller than him.

He didn't recall it being piled so high before, but there it was, and it was leaning.

"Oh no!" Walt gasped as the tower wobbled forward. He put his hands up in an attempt to stop it from falling, but suddenly it all tumbled towards him. As he was knocked to the floor by the weight of the clutter, he heard the unmistakable sounds of footsteps running for the back door. Within seconds he was pinned to the floor, with an assortment of papers, magazines, boxes, bedding, clothing, and countless other items piled on top of him. He struggled against the weight of it, but could not sit up or lift his arms. With the face mask over his mouth he struggled to breathe. Panic gripped him from the inside out. Sweat broke out over his skin. His brain crunched the numbers and he soon discovered that he would not live much longer. Between the weight of the clutter on top of him, and the limited air he could breathe, it could be anywhere from an hour, to mere minutes. Tears flooded his eyes as he realized that perhaps this was why he had been irritated by clutter for most of his life. Had some mystical and illogical part of him known that it would one day lead to his demise?

"I'm sorry, Jo," Walt whispered, as hot tears slid down his cheeks. "I'm sorry I didn't find you."

Walt heard another crash, and felt more weight added to the pile on his chest. He realized that the towers of clutter in the villa had begun to topple like dominoes. He closed his eyes and began to accept the fact that he would not be found for hours.

CHAPTER 17

"I'm sorry, Eddy, without the picture, I have no grounds to arrest him, yet. I will look at the picture on the recording of the show, but there is nothing I can do until I've verified it." Detective Cooper stood up from his desk and walked across the room to add some papers to a pile stacked on another table.

"That's ridiculous." Samantha threw her hands up in the air. "We know it was him. He had motive, he had opportunity—"

"And he wasn't even there!" Detective Cooper snapped. "Was he?" He looked between both of them. "Was his car on the surveillance video? Hmm? You two have been meddling so much, you should know, it wasn't!"

"You're right, it wasn't. But that doesn't mean he didn't walk in, Detective! You can't let yourself get zoned in on a few pieces of evidence, and miss out on the bigger picture!" Eddy snapped his fingers in front of the detective's face. "Wake up! We've found your killer, now you have to go get him!"

"Enough!" Detective Cooper pointed to the door. "Get out, both of you. I don't care if you have me fired. I have a job to do. I will look at the show again and speak to Brad if necessary, but it's not going to happen with you two here in my office. Go on!" He pointed to the door again.

Samantha sighed as she realized that they'd pushed too hard. Detective Cooper was no longer their ally.

"Let's go, Eddy."

"Yes, let's go." Eddy held open the door for her.

As Samantha started down the hallway towards the exit, Eddy caught her arm.

"I have one more stop to make. Can you call Walt for me? I want to know if he has heard from Jo."

"Sure." Samantha called Walt while Eddy disappeared inside of another office. A few minutes later he returned with a piece of paper, and grabbed

Samantha by the arm. "Hurry, let's go, I've got a lead. Did you reach Walt?"

"No, now he's not answering either." Samantha frowned. "Maybe we should go by his villa and grab him?"

"No, there's no time. I know where Brad is."

"Where?"

The pair walked quickly across the parking lot to Eddy's car. Once Samantha was settled, Eddy slammed on the gas. She could tell from the look in his eyes that nothing would deter him.

"Eddy, where are we going?"

"Chris was able to get me a location on Brad's cell phone. He's in Sage Gardens."

"What?" Samantha's eyes widened. "What would he be doing there?"

"I don't know, but I intend to find him before he slips away. I don't care what Detective Cooper says, there is enough evidence to make an arrest, and if not, then I'll get a confession out of him. I'm not going to let him get away with this. Here." Eddy tossed the piece of paper to her. "This was his last location. Keep your eyes peeled, all right?"

"All right." Samantha nodded. As she gazed through the window at the entrance of Sage

Gardens, she caught sight of a shiny blue car driving out. "Eddy!" She gasped. "There he is!"

"Are you sure?" Eddy twisted his head. "Are you sure it's him? The last location is closer to Shayla's villa."

"I think so. I think it was the same car." Samantha frowned as Eddy hit the brakes.

"But did you see his face, Sam?" Eddy shook his head. "We need to be sure."

"No, I didn't." Samantha sighed, then popped open the car door. "You go after the car, I'll go to Shayla's villa, it's not a far walk. We have to split up."

"Samantha." Eddy hesitated.

"Don't start that overprotective stuff with me right now." Samantha frowned and stepped out of the car.

"Fine, but be careful." Eddy frowned as she slammed the door shut.

"Just go after that car!" Samantha huffed as she looked over her shoulder at him.

As soon as Eddy took off, she started walking quickly. If Brad had gone to Shayla's villa then there was a good chance that he intended to sabotage any evidence he might have left behind. Had he set fire to it? Had he taken something that would have identified him as the killer? She felt more urgency as she drew closer to the villa. She started up the driveway when she noticed something in the grass. Her heart skipped a beat. It was a cell phone. Likely, Brad's cell phone. He probably dropped it on his way back to his car. Which meant she had proof that he was there. She left it where it was and headed for the villa. Maybe she could figure out what he'd done before further evidence of his murderous act could be destroyed. When she saw the door open, her heart skipped a beat. She peeked inside and saw that clutter had spilled into the hallway. She sighed as she realized that it would be impossible to find anything in such a mess.

The villa was a dead end. She could only hope that Eddy had been able to find Brad. If anyone could help her find some trace of evidence in the mess, it would be Walt. She called his cell and hoped that this time he would pick up. As she picked her way through the disaster, she listened to the rings in her ear. Then she heard something else. Walt's ringtone.

"What?" Samantha spun around in the direction of the sound. How could his phone be there? "Walt? Are you here?"

Samantha tried to follow the sound, but the

mounds of clutter blocked her way. As the call went to voicemail, the phone stopped ringing. Then she heard a subtle chirp that indicated a missed call. It came from under a huge pile of clutter.

"Walt!" Samantha gasped as she realized he might be trapped underneath of it. If he was, he wasn't able to answer her, which meant that she might already be too late. With tears in her eyes she called emergency on her phone and turned it on speaker phone. As she dug down through the endless items, she shouted her location, and the situation, into the phone. She knew she might need help in order to get to him.

"Walt, I'm here. I'm going to get you out!" Samantha gasped for breath as she dug even deeper. It would do no good to panic, but the thought of Walt trapped under the mass of clutter made her stomach churn. "Walt, can you hear me?"

Some of the clutter shifted and Samantha caught sight of what she thought might be the tip of Walt's perfectly shined shoe. She began throwing things over her shoulders as she dug as quickly as she could. Outside she heard sirens. She was relieved to know help was on the way, but she knew Walt needed it right at that moment. As she pulled away a folded blanket, she found his masked face. "Walt!"

Tears of relief stung her eyes as she pulled him up out of the remaining debris. "Can you breathe?" She tugged the mask free.

"Don't!" Walt gulped and put the mask back into position. "Years of dust has been shifted around in this space, do you know what that could do to a set of lungs?"

"Oh Walt!" Samantha threw her arms around him, despite the fact that he tended to avoid hugs.

"Sam, thank you for finding me." Walt hugged her in return, though pulled away quickly. "I really thought I was done for."

"Walt, Samantha?" Jo trudged down the hallway through the items that Samantha had just thrown.

"Jo!" Walt stumbled to his feet. "Jo, are you okay?"

"Of course I'm okay. Are you okay? I was at the police station when I heard the call for help come in." Jo looked between the two of them. "What happened?"

"Where were you?" Walt's eyes widened. "Did Detective Cooper arrest you?"

"No. Actually, I was helping Detective Cooper find Denver. I got Eddy's message and went straight to the police station, I had to act quickly before

Denver disappeared. I followed Denver and found out where he was staying. I told the detective where to find him. The vase was in his possession. I wanted to make sure he was off the streets. Apparently, it's a replica, but Denver didn't know that. While I was there, I heard about the emergency here. Walt, are you all right?" Jo lightly touched his shoulder. "You look so flushed."

"I am probably infested with dust mites, and all kinds of infections, but you're here, and safe, Jo. So yes, I'm okay." Walt gestured towards the door. "Let's get some fresh air."

"Take it slow, Walt, you may need to go to the hospital." Samantha frowned as she followed him.

"Are you kidding? Do you know how many germs are there? I'm fine." Walt took a deep breath of the fresh air. "Someone pushed all of that on me. Someone was in this house, and if you were with Denver then it couldn't have been him, Jo."

"No, it wasn't. It was Brad, and I've got his cell phone to prove it." Samantha pointed it out on the grass. "Eddy is hunting him down as we speak."

"Detective Cooper already picked him up." Eddy walked up the driveway towards them. "Is everyone okay?"

"We are." Walt nodded and finally took the mask

off his face. "I never want to experience something like that again."

"What's going on here?" Troy stepped out of his car, which was parked along the street. "What's all the commotion around my mother's villa?"

As Eddy walked over to fill him in on what had unfolded, Samantha spotted a little toy car in Troy's hand. She recognized it and her heart warmed at the sight of it. Troy hadn't taken the car to sell it, or to spite his mother, but because it was the very first one that she bought him. Despite their rough relationship, he still loved her. Samantha filled her friends in on what she and Eddy had discovered about Brad.

"Now, I understand." Walt turned to look at the house. "Often, with people that have compulsive disorders, there was some trauma that occurred that triggered or exacerbated the compulsion. I'm guessing that Shayla's guilt over lying to the police and protecting Brad from being arrested for murder, was the trigger that made her start collecting so excessively. I bet you she couldn't bring herself to throw the picture away and Brad was shocked she still had it."

"She's at peace now, at least." Samantha sighed.

"She is." Jo squinted at the villa. "I know I feel much better now that Denver is where he belongs."

"Me, too." Walt smiled at her. "And you were right, you didn't need me to keep you safe."

"That doesn't mean I don't appreciate the thought." Jo slung her arm around his shoulders. "Now Walt, what you need is a bath."

"In hand sanitizer." Walt nodded, then waved to Eddy as he walked over to them.

"Detective Cooper just sent me an update. Brad has been arrested for both murders. He admitted that Shayla had nothing to do with the first murder, she just went along with his alibi. She didn't want to believe he was guilty. Brad entered Sage Gardens on foot when he killed Shayla."

Samantha took one last look at the villa. Maybe, she hadn't been there to save Shayla, but at least with the help of her friends and Detective Cooper, she had managed to find justice for her.

The End

DUNE HOUSE COZY MYSTERIES

Seaside Secrets

Boats and Bad Guys

Treasured History

Hidden Hideaways

Dodgy Dealings

Suspects and Surprises

Ruffled Feathers

A Fishy Discovery

Danger in the Depths

Celebrities and Chaos

Pups, Pilots and Peril

Tides, Trails and Trouble

Racing and Robberies

Athletes and Alibis

CHOCOLATE CENTERED COZY MYSTERIES

The Sweet Smell of Murder

A Deadly Delicious Delivery

A Bitter Sweet Murder

A Treacherous Tasty Trail

Mistletoe, Makeup and Murder

Hairpin, Hair Dryer and Homicide

Blush, a Bride and a Body

Shampoo and a Stiff

Cosmetics, a Cruise and a Killer

Lipstick, a Long Iron and Lifeless

Camping, Concealer and Criminals

Treated and Dyed

A Wrinkle-Free Murder

A MACARON PATISSERIE COZY MYSTERY SERIES

Sifting for Suspects

Recipes and Revenge

Mansions, Macarons and Murder

NUTS ABOUT NUTS COZY MYSTERIES

A Tough Case to Crack

A Seed of Doubt

Roasted Penuts and Peril

HEAVENLY HIGHLAND INN COZY MYSTERIES

Murdering the Roses

Dead in the Daisies

Killing the Carnations

Drowning the Daffodils

Suffocating the Sunflowers

Books, Bullets and Blooms

A Deadly Serious Gardening Contest

A Bridal Bouquet and a Body

Digging for Dirt

WENDY THE WEDDING PLANNER COZY MYSTERIES

Matrimony, Money and Murder

Chefs, Ceremonies and Crimes

Knives and Nuptials

Mice, Marriage and Murder

ABOUT THE AUTHOR

Cindy Bell is a USA Today and Wall Street Journal Bestselling Author. She is the author of the cozy mystery series Wagging Tail, Donut Truck, Dune House, Sage Gardens, Chocolate Centered, Macaron Patisserie, Nuts about Nuts, Bekki the Beautician, Heavenly Highland Inn and Wendy the Wedding Planner.

Cindy has always loved reading, but it is only recently that she has discovered her passion for writing romantic cozy mysteries. She loves walking along the beach thinking of the next adventure her characters can embark on.

You can sign up for her newsletter so you are notified of her latest releases at http://www.cindybellbooks.com.

Made in United States
North Haven, CT
26 December 2023

46673246R00124